NUMBER 12 RUE SAINTE-CATHERINE

AND OTHER STORIES

ROBERTA HARTLING GATES

RUNNING WILD

RUNNING WILD PRESS

Number 12 Rue Sainte-Catherine
text copyright © 2024 Reserved by Roberta Hartling Gates
Edited by Benjamin White

Paperback ISBN: 978-1-960018-90-8
eBook ISBN: 978-1-960018-28-1

The following stories have been previously published:

"Mama's Boy" (*Slippery Elm*)
"On Special Assignment" (*Beloit Fiction Journal*)
"Number 12 Rue Sainte-Catherine" (*The Write Launch*)
"Collaboration" (*Night Picnic*)
"The Making of a Martyr" (*Solstice*)
"The Man Who Wore Violets" (*Soundings Review*)
"Bullyboys" (*Punt Volat*)

For my mother, Irene Hartling

CONTENTS

MAMA'S BOY

UDLER, GERMANY - 1920

Klaus was cursed with a father who was omnipresent. At home, he was there, nagging, belittling, bellowing. Then at school, there he was again, just as belligerent and just as loud, because it was his job to maintain discipline, that's what they paid him for.

Order and discipline, that was his mantra. Even stumbling around drunk, he'd invoke the words. "Order, that's what we need in this house," he'd yell in the direction of Klaus's mother, who pretended not to hear. Or, if it was at school, he'd pound on his teacher's desk and bark out, "Order and discipline: that's what you boys need. Just wait till you're in the army, they'll take care of you *Waschlappen*." Sissies, that was what he called them, either that or mama's boys, something else he could not abide.

Klaus knew he was a mama's boy, one of the worst probably, but nothing his father could say made any difference. He stuck as closely as he could to his mother, running to her for kisses, bringing her his scraped knees, hanging about the kitchen like a cast-away puppy. She'd give him her tired smile and ask him to do some small thing: open the fire box on the stove and stir up the coals, or fetch a stool and get something down from the top shelf of a cupboard, a pickle dish, say, or a mixing bowl—No, not that one, the yellow one with the aqua stripe, yes, that's it, that's the one. It made Klaus happy to do these small things for his mother. She didn't complain, that would have been a weakness, but Klaus could see how cornered she was: on one side, a husband who yelled, on the other, Kurt, his little brother, who was an embarrassment to everybody but himself—a foolish child who spent his days grinning and drooling.

After a school day spent with his father, being in the presence of his mother came as a relief to Klaus. It hardly mattered what she was doing—making noodles, pickling beets, cleaning a chicken—he was happy just to be there, close to her. But if someone had asked him, Now, tell me, son, what days are best?, he would have answered without hesitation that pie days were the best. His mother was renowned for her pies—they were always in demand, especially for funerals—and Klaus never grew tired of watching her make them (she didn't bother with a recipe, never stopped to measure anything, she just *knew*). The dough, conjured up out of practically nothing—just flour and lard, a sprinkling of water—was particularly wondrous, and he loved to watch her quick slim hands forming it into a ball, then pushing it this way and that with her porcelain rolling pin, stretching it out, thinner and thinner, until it finally assumed a circular shape no thicker than a sheet of paper. Next, in one quick motion, so quick it was almost a sleight of hand, she'd fold the circle into quarters, drop it into a waiting tin and unfurl it so smoothly, so neatly that it might have been done by machine. Then, finally, she'd balance the pan on the fingertips of one hand, while using the other to knock a knife against the rim, all the way around, to trim off the excess.

Klaus didn't know what other mothers did with these trimmings, but his always saved them and turned them into a treat for him (well, also for Kurt, if he happened to be there). She'd gather up the leftover pieces and spread them out on a cookie sheet, while Klaus mixed sugar and cinnamon to sprinkle over them—which he did with a flourish, pretending to be a priest sprinkling holy water. In the meantime, she'd crimp the edge of the pie shell with her forefinger and thumb while asking him about the shapes of the pieces: *That one, for instance, what did it remind him of?*

"It's a cloud," he'd declare, more or less guided by its roundish shape, and she'd laugh.

"Oh, Klaus, you could say that about all of them. See if you can come up with something more original."

So he'd try again: "Well, it might be a pillow."

His mother would frown–well, not frown exactly, but somehow indicate that his answer was lacking–and then his nincompoop brother would barge in even though he and Mutti were having a private conversation. "Haystack," Kurt would say, putting his sticky fingers all over the dough and looking pleased with himself. Mutti would smile then and call him *mein guter Junge*, and that was that: there was no stopping him then. "Ice cream, fat face, mushy peas . . ." he'd lisp, babbling away like the idiot he was. Klaus couldn't stand his showing off, but he tried hard to ignore it, because once, when he'd gotten mad and kicked Kurt out of the way, Mutti had given him such a horrified look that all he could do was slink away and hide. If she'd boxed his ears or slapped him silly, it wouldn't have been so bad, he could have stood that. But his mother didn't believe in hitting. She wouldn't hit back even if she was the one being hit.

All of this made Klaus wonder why his mother had chosen to marry a man like his father. Had he always been this way?

Or had there been a time when he was different? By "different," Klaus didn't mean kind or sensitive, only predictable and ordinary, like the farmer-fathers his classmates went home to, men who seemed content to work hard, have their one stein of beer at the pub, and then go to bed early. But when Klaus asked his mother about this on one of their pie days, he could see how reluctant she was to answer him.

For several long moments, Anna let Klaus's question hang there, but then, pressing her lips together, she put down her rolling pin and turned to gaze at her son. He was such a sweet boy, delicate almost, and small for his age. But why, Lord, did he need to know about these things? Why, at age eight, take on all that ballast? But he had asked, and she was the sort of woman who believed you should respect children enough to answer their questions.

She wiped her hands on her apron and knelt before him. "Papi does love you, you know that, don't you?" she said, taking his hands in hers, and he nodded, urged on, she supposed, by the tone of her voice. "It's just his wound that's the problem. It hurts him and then he gets cross." She paused then, listening for a moment to the long clock in the hall, whose ticking sounded like the snapping of twigs. "It's not something he can help," she went on, squeezing his little-boy hands and almost breaking into tears when he nodded again. She knew what he wanted—to be claimed, fully and benevolently, by his father— but she also knew, better than anyone else, how impossible that was. Klaus Sr. had not agreed to marry her until the baby she'd been carrying was three months old, by which time it was too late. Now, because of those negligent three months, her son, in the eyes of the law and everyone else, would always be illegitimate.

She sighed and stood up, feeling worn-out and useless. Did she have nothing better than a cinnamon crisp to offer her son?

"If only he hadn't been injured," she said, permitting herself, just for a moment, to contemplate other possibilities, "or if the doctors had been able to do something for him, but . . ." Her voice trailed off then and she gazed out the window to where the sun was being pulled down beneath the brow of the horizon. "That's why he drinks," she added. "Because otherwise he wouldn't be able to stand it."

For days Klaus tried to make sense of what his mother had told him, but then he gave up: it was all too baffling. How could this single injury, bad as it was, be an adequate explanation for all the cruelties his father bestowed, one after the other, as indifferently as a machine? After all, lots of fathers had come home from the war with injuries. You saw them everywhere, crutches swinging, coat sleeves empty. Take their neighbor Herr Koeppen: he had to do everything one-handed, but did he gripe about it? No, he just got on with things. Sometimes you'd even see him joking around with the other men on Sundays after mass. Yet his father, Udler's testy schoolmaster, could not get through a day—or even an hour—without clutching his throat and groaning like a stuck pig. It was almost automatic. When Christoph, the class dunce, stood at the board, staring into a long division problem that he would never solve, Klaus's father would grip his neck and groan. When Mutti suggested— and that's all it was, just a suggestion—that he bring up some coal from the schoolhouse cellar, his hand would fly to his throat and another groan would come out of him.

Klaus wondered what it would be like to get shot, to have a piece of hot lead sink into the soft dough of your body, but he could never imagine it. Nor did he understand why the doctors hadn't operated. His mother said that they'd probably been afraid to, that an operation like that would have been too risky. Or they might have been overwhelmed, who knew? Or maybe they'd thought, or at least hoped, that his body would seal off the damage on its own, the way skin and hair cover over the places where a bull's horns used to be. But Mutti said that his father's wound wasn't like that, that it had been stubborn and refused to heal. She said that even now, two years after he'd made his way home from the trenches, it still hadn't closed completely.

Klaus knew it was wrong to wonder about something his father so clearly regarded as secret and shameful, but Klaus couldn't help it. Daily, the idea grew in him that this injury, this unhealed wound of his father's, might explain everything. If he saw it for himself, then he might understand. He bided his time, waiting until one Saturday in November when the house was empty except for his father who was "napping." Sprawled across the sofa with arms and legs dangling, his father looked huge, like an ape who had stumbled in from the jungle and fallen into a stupor. Afraid that this beast of a man might come to at any moment and start roaring, Klaus was cautious: a slow creep across the linoleum floor, then a long and frozen moment spent crouching at his father's side while he listened to his snorts and snarls, trying to determine how deeply asleep he was.

Klaus glanced at the clock: his mother and Kurt would be home soon, in another ten minutes perhaps, twenty at most. If he was going to do this, it had to be now. Taking a long breath and bracing himself, he peeled back the high celluloid collar his father wore (how stiff it was, how hard) and peered at the long irregular scar underneath. It was a purplish-pink color, bumpy and contorted like a worm, with a thick gauze pad stuck to one end.

So this was it: The Wound that everyone had to bow down to. Frightened that his *betrunken* father would awaken at any moment and start swatting at him with his long arms, Klaus cautiously picked at the edge of the bandage until, finally, he was able to dislodge the gauze pad. Beneath it, a gaping hole not much larger than the thin end of a funnel stared back at him. It was grotesque, a reddish raw color, with a smooth wide mouth that seemed to open and close almost as if it were breathing. Mesmerized, Klaus watched as pus oozed out of the hole with every "breath," congealing into a sticky yellowish jelly that looked like snot. He bent his face close—but not too close!—and sniffed, recognizing the unaccounted-for smell of his father. Like most of the men who lived in Udler, his father carried with him the odors of tobacco, animal dung and alcohol, though in his case the alcohol smell was damper and heavier, almost as if he were being pickled. Hidden somewhere in the background, though, was something else, another smell that Klaus had unconsciously puzzled over. And now here it was, right beneath his nose, the indisputable evidence of the rot that festered in his father.

The man was a walking pustule, an ogre who carried contagion with him like a cloud. And he was that man's son. He might not be acknowledged, might never be able to inherit, yet somehow, he knew that his father's stink would always be with him. Even now, he could feel it being transferred to him, inexorably seeping into his clothes, his hair, his skin. And in that moment, it came to him, not in words or as an actual idea, but as a truth he no longer resisted, that this—and this alone—would be his inheritance.

UNCLE KARL

TRIER, GERMANY - 1929

When he heard his father waking up—first coughing and spitting, then staggering to the bathroom where he stood over the bowl groaning as he tried to pee—Klaus had only one objective: to get out of the flat as fast as he could. Forget changing his underwear, yesterday's would have to do, and his books—where were they? Yes, there on the kitchen table—but he didn't have time for breakfast. He felt bad for Mutter who'd gotten up early to make him cocoa, but a quick kiss was all he could spare her. Then he was pounding down the stairs feeling guilty and inadequate, nearly tripping in his eagerness to get away. It was so awful, the way his mother had no one but him.

But Mutter understood, he knew she did. He had to stay out of Vater's way as much as he could, or else there'd never be a moment's peace. It had been bad enough when his father was working, but now that he'd been relieved of his duties (too many canings, the parents had said), it was even worse.

Half-walking, half-running up Fahrstrasse, Klaus wished he could do something to make his mother's life better. He at least had school, but she had to be at home all day, a slave not just to his father, but also to Kurt, that imbecile brother of his.

Who knew what Vater would make her do: bring him breakfast in bed, change his putrid dressing, parcel out the vodka that was killing him.

Taking care of Kurt was easier. He was so simple, like a four-year-old, playing with his toy soldiers and humming to himself. But then Kurt was in the habit of soiling himself, which made all sorts of extra work for Mutter. And she liked a clean house, she did! Everything might be old, but she wanted it spotless.

Klaus kicked at the dry leaves in his path. He hoped he wouldn't be called on to recite in Latin class. He was generally pretty good at Latin, but the passage Dr. Kutcher had assigned for today was a tough one. Mutter had tried to help—she'd been a teacher just like his father, so she liked going over his lessons with him—but that had been too much for Vater.

"You good-for-nothing loafer," he'd yelled, swiping at Klaus with his cane. "And you," he added, throwing Mutter a dark look, "you think you're so smart, so commendable sitting here doing your son's homework for him."

Klaus looked up at the bluish-black clouds which hung above him and wondered if he'd seen a dark spot on Mutter's cheek that morning. They had to save on electricity so the kitchen was always dim, and he'd been in a hurry of course, so it might have been nothing, a smudge perhaps, or even a shadow. But he knew that wasn't right. As usual, there could be only one explanation: His monster father had been at it again, actually hitting her in the face this time, not because she'd done anything, but just because she was there.

Mutter never complained, though. She excused him because he was sick and in pain, but Klaus knew she was ashamed. It was why she wore long-sleeved dresses even in summer, pinning the collars closed whenever she went to the market or early morning mass so that no one would know. Klaus wasn't supposed to know either, but how could he not? His father did the same to him, attacking when he least expected it, yanking him out of bed even, and hitting him everywhere except on the face, having that much restraint at least because he didn't want the priests at school asking questions.

When Klaus got to Jesuitenstrasse, he paused briefly to take in the sight of his school, something he did almost every morning.

Dating from the 1500s, The Friedrich-Wilhelm-Gymnasium looked more like a palace than a school, and Klaus had a deep reverence, both for its architecture and for the regulated way things were run. Classes always progressed in an orderly fashion, and everyone was bound by the same set of immutable rules.

No one at the school—not his teachers, not his classmates—knew what Klaus endured at home, so here he could pass as normal. He was just another student, an ordinary kid with a talent for soccer and a modest gift for languages. Not a class leader maybe, but well enough liked to blend in, which was all he really wanted.

The heavy wrought iron gate which led to the grounds was still locked, but Klaus didn't mind. He was used to waiting. Leaning against the red brick wall which surrounded the property, he glanced at the heavy clouds overhead and hoped it wouldn't rain before he could get inside. It would no doubt be too wet for soccer today, so chances were they'd have to make do with handball in the gym. But that was all right—handball was fun too—and then after school, if he felt like it, he might run over to the Brown House to see how Uncle Karl was doing.

Herr Horrmann wasn't a real uncle of course, but it was

what he liked to be called. He was the group leader in Trier, a big red-headed man who always had some small assignment for Klaus whenever he stopped by. *Get these files sorted out so they're in alphabetical order,* he'd say, or *Take down this message and run it over to Hauser, you know where he is, over at the butcher shop around the corner.* Klaus was happy to do these things, it made him feel useful and important. His mother (he'd told her a little bit about these errands) had asked him if he was being paid. When he'd said no, she'd pressed her lips together so they made a straight line, but she hadn't said anything else. She hadn't told him not to go there.

* * *

All morning long the rain came down in torrents, glazing the cobblestoned streets and turning whatever leaves were left on the trees into water-soaked rags. After lunch, though, just in time for Latin, the sun came out. Suddenly the homeroom sparkled: the windows, the varnished floor, and—brightest of all —the big brass crucifix which hung over the blackboard.

Dr. Kutcher entered the room carrying an old pickle jar full of the students' names. "*Guten Tag, Klasse,*" he said in his blasé way.

"*Guten Tag,* Dr. Kutcher," the boys shouted in unison, jumping to their feet like cadets. Dr. Kutcher was not much to look at—a tall, stork-like man who was thin all over except for his round ball of a belly—but he'd been at Friedrich-Wilhelm for years, for decades actually, and he was tough. There was no getting anything past him.

Dr. Kutcher picked up a thin wooden pointer from the chalk tray and rapped it on the top of his desk to get everyone's attention. Klaus exchanged a quick look with his seatmate, Konrad: perhaps they'd get lucky today and escape Dr. Kutcher's attention. Two stanzas, twenty lines in all, from Ovid's *Metamorphoses*, that had been their assignment, which they had to be able to read in Latin, then translate into German.

Dr. Kutcher pulled the first name out of his pickle jar. It was Schilling, a big sleepy-eyed boy whose shoulders were so broad that, if you saw him from the back, you'd think he was a man. He was not much of a student, though. Four lines was the best he could do and even those were rough.

"Sit down," Dr. Kutcher growled, shooting him the kind of look that would have killed a cat. Becker was the next victim. He was a thin nervous boy who did well on written exams but lost his footing whenever he had to recite in class. He managed to get through a dozen lines but had to start over twice and his pronunciation was hit-and-miss.

Klaus glanced again at Konrad, just another quick look, involuntary really, but Dr. Kutcher saw it and that was enough. Pushing his pickle jar aside, he bore in on Klaus. "You there, Barbie, you go next," he said.

Klaus stood up, painfully aware that he was only half-prepared. But at least he could do the first stanza. Mutter had helped him with that one. *"In nova fet animus mutates dicere formas corpora,"* he intoned as he bent his head over the book, not reading the words so much as letting the sounds of them run over his tongue. His pronunciation wasn't perfect, but it didn't matter. He was reading so fast that there wasn't time for Herr Kutcher to step in and correct him.

And the translation went equally well. "My mind takes me to speak of forms changed into new bodies," he began, letting Mutter's words come back to him in a stream. Out of the corner of his eye, he could see Konrad following along with his finger and nodding his head in tacit approval as Klaus glided through the stanza, so confident that when he got to "bring down perpetual song," which were the ending words, he couldn't resist giving them a flourish.

Klaus looked up from his book and then, without meaning to, surveyed the room, which was unusually quiet. His classmates were impressed, Klaus could tell.

But Dr. Kutcher quickly broke the spell. "And the second stanza?" he asked. "You haven't forgotten it, have you?"

Klaus looked down at his book to see the second stanza swimming up to greet him. It was true that he *had* momentarily forgotten about it, but what could he do now? He'd just have to do his best. He cleared his throat and started reading aloud in Latin, his mouth so dry he could barely shape the words. Somehow, though, he managed to stumble through to the end. But that was the most he could do. If he had to attempt a translation, he'd probably throw up instead.

Cautiously, Klaus looked up at Dr. Kutcher, admitting defeat with a minute shrug of his shoulders. All he wanted at that moment was just to sit down and have done with it, no matter how bad the tongue-lashing.

But Klaus should have known better than to hope for clemency. While Dr. Kutcher wasn't cruel, not as bad as some anyway, he was one of those teachers who believed that everything, once started, should be finished. If you were able to read a passage through to the end, then you needed to translate it too.

"And the meaning?" he asked.

Klaus stared at the first line of the stanza—*Ante mare et terrās et quod tegit omnia caelum*—and tried to beat back his panic. What could it mean? He had no idea. But then, slowly, he realized that *"Ante mare et terrās"* had to mean . . .

"Before the sea and the lands," he blurted out, momentarily relieved to have come up with something. Unfortunately, though, it was all he could do. The rest was a mystery, an impenetrable mush.

But then, out of the corner of his eye, Klaus saw Konrad nudging his book in his direction, pointing with his index finger to the next words and, just above them, the translations he'd penciled in.

Klaus glimpsed one word only—*caelum*, meaning sky—but then looked away fast. He was not a cheater!

But it was too late, Dr. Kutcher had noticed. He banged his stick down on his desk so hard that everyone jumped. "How dare you cheat in my class," he roared, scowling at Klaus. "I won't have it, not from you or anyone else."

Klaus tried to explain himself. "But, Dr. Kutcher, I didn't see any—" he started, but it was pointless. Dr. Kutcher was making so much noise with his stick that nothing else could be heard.

"In the hall, please," he said, his face the color of raw liver as he pointed Klaus toward the doorway with his stick. "The Rector will deal with you later."

* * *

Klaus took off running the minute he was dismissed from the Rector's office. Propelling himself against the wind, he could feel his eyes stinging as he headed for the Brown House. If he'd ever considered becoming a priest—and he had, as recently as last year—those thoughts were banished now.

He simply couldn't get over the Rector and how scornful he'd been, sitting there surrounded by all that luxury of his: heavy velvet drapes at the window, a thick Persian rug underfoot, oil paintings in heavy gilt frames on each of the walls. He might as well have been the pope. Even more disgusting was the way he listened to everything Dr. Kutcher had to say, just lapping it up, while all he could do was lift an eyebrow when it was Klaus's turn to tell his side of things. And, really, was his story so hard to believe? He hadn't known Konrad would try to help him, they hadn't made plans ahead of time. And besides, he hadn't looked—well, maybe just for a moment—but even if he had, he hadn't seen anything.

But the Rector wasn't interested in the truth. Looking down his long nose at Klaus, he dispatched him with a demerit and a long-winded lecture about making a good confession. Klaus could take whatever was dished out to him (his father had taught him that much), but what about Mutter? She'd be so disappointed in him. And what if he was held back for a year because of this? It would be just one more thing that she'd have to endure.

*　*　*

When he got to the Brown House, Klaus saw that the door to Uncle Karl's office was closed. Obviously, he was busy with someone else, probably one of his Stormtroopers. There were always a lot of them in the building, rushing around acting important, but just what they did beyond marching and picking fights, Klaus wasn't sure. They could be nasty, though, he knew that much. Just last month, while watching a procession of them go by on the street, he'd seen one of them leap out of formation and slash a heckler's face open with his knife.

Guessing the wait might be long, Klaus thought about going home, but before he could make up his mind, a scrawny kid wearing a swastika armband burst through the door practically knocking him over. He couldn't have been more than a couple of years older than Klaus, but he had a tough, brutish look that reminded Klaus of the prisoners he'd met since joining the *Männerfursorgeverein*. Klaus wasn't all that keen on visiting jails or handing out New Testaments, but he'd stuck with it because the *Männerfursorgeverein* was the kind of do-gooder organization his father couldn't abide.

Klaus stepped up to Uncle Karl's door and knocked tentatively. He thought Uncle Karl might be too busy to see him, but when he came to the door he was all smiles. "Ah, Klaus," he said, clapping him on the shoulder. "I was just thinking about you."

"If you're busy, I can come back some other—" Klaus began, but Uncle Karl interrupted him.

"No, of course not. I'm glad you came by." He gestured toward the wooden chair in front of his desk and Klaus sat down, feeling almost at home. Everything here was so familiar to him he hardly gave it a thought: Uncle Karl's big oak desk, the portrait of Hitler which hung behind it in a plain wood frame, and, just off to the side, a Nazi flag which stood in a holder on the floor. The rest of the room—bare walls, bare floors—was simple, the exact opposite of the Rector's.

"So how're things?" asked Uncle Karl, leaning back in his swivel chair and lacing his hands behind his head.

Klaus shrugged. "All right," he said tonelessly.

Uncle Karl looked at him closely. "Just all right, that's it?" he said, keeping his tone casual. "Did something happen? Something at school maybe?"

Klaus shrugged again and looked down at his boots. He had no intention of divulging any detail of his run-in with the Rector.

But Uncle Karl, who seemed to intuit the situation, managed to guess what Klaus wasn't saying.

"I knew it," he said, sounding outraged on Klaus's behalf. "Honestly, the way they run things over at Friedrich-Wilhelm I wouldn't be surprised if you were fed up with the whole kit and kaboodle." He tipped his chair forward and laid his heavy forearms on the desk. "Grouchy old teachers. Fathers always looking over your shoulder. Routine for routine's sake." He glanced knowingly at Klaus. "And the Rector, he's the worst of all, isn't he?"

Klaus, close to tears, sat without moving. The two of them had never talked about school before, or not much anyway. But clearly Uncle Karl understood how things were.

"He gave me a demerit today," said Klaus, unable to hold in his secret any longer.

"Who? The Rector?"

Klaus nodded miserably. "He said I was cheating."

"What, a good kid like you?" asked Uncle Karl, shaking his head. "That's ridiculous."

Klaus was stunned. Except for Mutter, no one ever called him good. No one ever took his side. "But I didn't do it," he exclaimed. "Maybe it looked that way, but I would never—"

"Of course you wouldn't," said Uncle Karl. He picked up a paperclip and began to unbend it. "That's the way it is in places like that. The rich kids skate through, nothing ever sticks to them, but the poor kids, one little mistake, one hair out of place, and that's it, they're crucified."

Klaus sat stupefied, his eyes fixed on the paperclip Uncle Karl was straightening out. He had never thought of the Gymnasium in this way. There were boys who were smart, boys who were religious, boys who were athletic—and of course *they* rose in the ranks, it was to be expected—but boys who were rich? Suddenly he saw things in a new light.

"Makes you mad, doesn't it," said Uncle Karl, "the way a privileged few get all the luck." He tossed the straightened paperclip into a nearby wastebasket where it landed with a metallic clank.

"I don't know," muttered Klaus, unwilling to condemn the school that, until today, he had loved with all his heart.

"Yes, you do know," said Uncle Karl, sounding almost angry. "People like that, even religious people who've taken orders, they're just as fixated on money and power as anybody else." For a moment or two, he looked intently at Klaus. "You do see that, don't you?"

Klaus shifted uneasily in his chair. He had no idea where Uncle Karl was going with this, but he could see how worked up he was getting.

"Don't believe me?" said Uncle Karl, his face and neck reddening. "Then ask yourself who's behind the Zentrum party. It's the Church of course."

Klaus didn't know what to say. Even though the Zentrum party was called the *Catholic* Zentrum party, he'd never thought of it as anything but a bunch of politicians. The idea that someone like the Rector, who looked almost medieval in his soutane, was pulling levers behind the scenes struck him as absurd.

"People don't want to believe it," said Uncle Karl, thrusting out his jaw defiantly, "but this city is a hotbed of clerical opposition. Forget patriotism, forget duty, the only thing the Church cares about is the status quo." His eyes bore into Klaus's. "But where is the status quo getting us? People like you and me are still struggling, nobody can get ahead."

Klaus thought of his own home where everything was worn out: chipped dishes, mismatched cutlery, rugs so thin you couldn't see their pattern anymore.

"But Hitler is going to change things," Uncle Karl continued, turning a little in his chair and waving at the portrait of Hitler behind him as if he knew the man personally. "Just wait, he'll clean out the rot here in Trier. Then little people like us will actually have a chance."

Outside, the evening traffic was picking up. Horns were honking, newsboys were busy hawking their newspapers on street corners. But Klaus barely noticed. He was stuck on the notion that Uncle Karl seemed to think he was one of those little people who didn't have a chance. "But I'm at the Gymnasium," he said. "When I get my *Abitur*, I can go on to—"

"You think you can go on to university? You honestly think that?" asked Uncle Karl, interrupting him. "Sure, you can qualify," he added, his tone more like the Rector's now, "but can your parents afford it? I mean, that's the question, isn't it?"

Klaus felt as if something he'd always counted on was slipping away from him. He knew his parents were poor, but they'd managed to pay the Gymnasium fees, hadn't they? It had made him think—well, he'd just sort of assumed—that somehow, when the time came . . .

Across from him, Uncle Karl barked out a laugh. "Oh, come now, Klaus, there's no need to look so glum," he said, sounding more amused than sympathetic.

Instantly Klaus felt his face flush with anger. This was the third time that day that he'd been cut down by his elders: first Dr. Kutcher, then the Rector—and now even Uncle Karl.

"That's easy for you to say," he said, looking straight at Uncle Karl. "You've found a place for yourself. But what about someone like me? What do I have to look forward to—nothing!"

Uncle Karl seemed a little startled by this outburst. "No, that's not true. Better days are coming, I promise you."

"What, because of the Nazis?" sneered Klaus.

"Yes, because of the Nazis, as you call them," said Uncle Karl, his face fierce with belief. "As soon as they're in power, everything will change. Germany will get back on its feet, you'll see. Then, if you want to be a lawyer, you can be a lawyer. The party will help you."

Klaus looked at Uncle Karl skeptically. "Who says I want to be a lawyer?"

"You did. Several months ago, right here in this office."

It was true, Klaus remembered the conversation all too well. It had been at Easter-time and Uncle Karl had been especially nice that day, asking him all sorts of questions about himself and his plans for the future.

"Well, so what if I did? It's a lost cause now. That's what you just said, isn't it?"

"No, what I said was that the party would—"

"Oh, sure," scoffed Klaus. "The party that got only three percent of the vote in the last election, they'll be able to help me."

For a moment Uncle Karl was quiet, as if restraining himself. "All right, Klaus," he finally said, "so maybe that's the situation now, but think ahead to the future. Müller's coalition is going to fall apart sooner or later and when it does, the Nationalists will be there to pick up the pieces. And they'll be looking for people like you: eager, ambitious, devoted to the cause. But you'll need to be ready," he warned. "There won't be a place for laggards."

Klaus, a little overcome by all this heady talk, shifted his gaze to the portrait of Hitler. There was no expression on his face, and the uniform he wore looked made up. But it would have to be made up, Klaus reflected, because Hitler had never been anything more than a lowly corporal. Even his own father had done better than that. He'd been a sergeant.

Klaus swung his eyes back to Uncle Karl. "What do you mean by ready?" he asked.

Almost instantly Uncle Karl seemed to relax. The tension went out of his arms and face and he seemed almost jolly. "Oh, just helping us out with a few things, that's all."

"I thought I already helped you," said Klaus, thinking of all those errands he'd run for free.

"Well, yes, that's certainly true," said Uncle Karl. He ran a hand over his closely cropped head. "And we're grateful of course. But I'm talking about something else. Something more meaningful."

Klaus had no idea what he was talking about. "Like what?" he asked.

"Well, you belong to the *Catholitsche Jugend*, don't you?" asked Uncle Karl, aiming his big gap-toothed smile right at Klaus.

* * *

Lying awake that night in his bed with the sagging mattress, Klaus watched the shadows flit across the ceiling and thought about what Uncle Karl had said.

It might seem like snitching, he'd said, but it wasn't, not really. "Think of it more as 'opposition research,'" he told Klaus, claiming that it was something all political parties did. And besides, he wasn't going to ask Klaus for anything big, just tidbits from here and there— "trends," as he put it.

Klaus had been too tangled up in his thoughts to promise anything—in fact, he'd hardly said anything at all—but Uncle Karl seemed to understand. He said Klaus should go home and think about it, that it wasn't the sort of decision you rushed into. "Just weigh the pros and cons," he said, making it sound straightforward and easy.

But it wasn't easy.

Informing on his teachers and classmates—the idea was repellent. No schoolboy would ever accede to that. Even if there was a good reason for blabbing—a health reason, say, like Konrad's passing out in gym class—you still kept your mouth shut. Teachers, of course, were different. You couldn't expect reciprocity from them—they could say whatever they liked to your parents or anyone else—but the thought of spying on them, of jotting down every little thing they said was unthinkable. Even if Uncle Karl was right and this was the opportunity of a lifetime, Klaus knew he'd never be able to make himself do it. Just the thought of it made him sick.

Klaus was half-asleep when he was jolted awake by the noises coming from his parents' bedroom: first the sound of something heavy crashing to the floor (the lamp probably) and then his father's voice spewing venom.

Klaus knew the rules, they hadn't changed since he was a little boy—just stay put and pretend nothing is happening—but he could tell by the way his father was carrying on that this wasn't a routine squabble. He crept to his door and listened.

Apparently Mutter had dumped out Vater's booze, that was the problem, and now he was calling her all sorts of vile and horrible things—*dumm Kuh* and *Hure* and even *Fotze*. "Dumb cow" and "whore," those were bad enough, but "cunt" —how dare he call her that. It was disgusting.

Forgetting the rules, forgetting everything really, Klaus hurried down the narrow hallway to his parents' room. Before, he'd heard only his father's voice, but now he could make out his mother's too, low and cajoling, pleading with his father to *Please, just get into bed and be quiet.*

For a moment Klaus stood in front of their door paralyzed. Entering his parents' bedroom had always been *verboten,* but then his mother cried out—it was a raw, loose sound stripped of words—and that was it, he couldn't hide himself any longer. Banging open the door, he saw his father standing off to one side in a sleeveless undershirt with his suspenders undone and his fists clenched. At his feet lay the ginger jar lamp, its base broken into pieces.

A malevolent expression flickered across his father's face. "Get out of here," he snarled, gesturing for Klaus to leave. "No one wants you here, don't you know that?"

But Klaus wasn't listening. His attention was fixed on

Mutter who was huddled in a corner looking small—so small, like a child almost—with blood dripping from her nose onto her nightdress. Reluctantly, she looked up at Klaus, her face slack with regret, and in that instant he understood: she didn't want him to witness this—it was her cross to bear alone.

Klaus turned to face his father. "You're a monster, you know that?" he shouted. He had never said anything like that to his father before, but the words had been there for a long time, ready to come out. "A monster!" he repeated. "And if you had any decency, you'd die right now and put everybody out of their misery."

His father laughed his stupid drunk laugh. "So you're the big man now, is that it?"

For a moment Klaus looked him over. His father had been powerful once, but he was pathetic now, as withered and stringy as an old carrot.

"Well, what're you waiting for?" taunted his father. "Let's see what you've got."

Something inside Klaus came loose then and he lunged forward, slamming his fist into the side of his father's head so hard that it sent him thudding against the wall. Vater put up his arms in an effort to bat Klaus away, but the more he tried to defend himself, the more alive Klaus felt. Not all of his blows connected, but then he got in a good one, slugging his father so deep in the stomach that the air went out of him in a *Whoosh!* and he slid down the wall to the floor.

Klaus, feeling a sudden surge of satisfaction, stepped back and stared at his father. It came as a shock to see how old he had gotten. His hair was almost completely gray now, his skin so baggy and loose it looked rubbery. And what a bluffer, not one punch thrown, just nothing at all.

Klaus glanced at his mother.

"We have to get him up," she said, meeting his gaze. Her

nose was still bleeding, but she sounded like herself again, pragmatic and capable, a woman who knew how to clean up messes.

But Klaus resisted. "No, just leave him there. It's what he deserves."

Mutter looked at him sharply. "Leave him here all night?" she asked. "Surely you don't mean that."

Klaus was dumbfounded. This was the ogre who had made his childhood a nightmare, who had sucked every bit of joy out of his mother's life for the past sixteen years, and yet she thought he deserved sympathy?

"So he sleeps on the floor one night, so what?" said Klaus.

Mutter glanced at her husband who sat on the floor clutching his belly and moaning. "Klaus, please, just help me," she said, half-commanding, half pleading as she turned her gaze on him. "There's no way I can do this by myself."

Klaus thought that his father was probably faking it, that if he wanted to he could pick himself up and stumble across the room to bed, but he relented because he was a good son who was in the habit of doing what his mother asked him to. Wedging his hands under Vater's armpits, Klaus managed to hoist him off the floor. Then Mutter picked him up by the feet and together they lugged him across the room and dumped him onto the bed like a sack of grain.

Reflexively, Mutter dusted her hands, then stood there looking at the shards of blue-and-white porcelain which littered the floor. Klaus knew how much she had liked the lamp. It had been a wedding gift from one of her sisters.

"Do you want me to get the broom and dustpan?" he asked, but she shook her head.

"No, I will," she said in a tone of resignation. "Just stay here till I get back," she added, leaving Klaus in the place he least wanted to be: alone with his father. Not knowing what else to do with himself, Klaus started to pace, over to the window, then back toward the bed, careful always to keep his eyes off his father. The room was ominously quiet, just the tick of the clock, the ragged sound of his father's breathing.

Klaus was on his fifth trip across the room toward the bed, when his father reached out abruptly and grabbed him by the arm.

"Proud of yourself, are you?" he rasped. His eyes were red and bleary, and there was a purplish lump on his temple. "We deny ourselves everything just to keep you at the Gymnasium, and this is how you repay us?"

Klaus was incredulous. "Deny yourself everything? Really?" he asked, shaking off his father's grasp which was surprisingly strong. "Mutter hasn't had any new clothes in I don't know how long, and we never have meat—I can't even remember when the last time was—but *you*," he added, pointing an index finger at his father, "*you* always manage to keep yourself in vodka."

"A lot you know about anything," growled his father. "You've never had to sleep in a trench full of mud or wake up in the night with rats running over your—"

"Oh, the war," jeered Klaus, interrupting him. "It was awful, you've told me a hundred times. But it doesn't excuse you. It doesn't." He was incensed now, even shaking a little. "Everybody else's father that I know of was in the war, too, but they don't act the way you do. They're not in a drunken stupor all day, they don't yank their kids out of bed at night to give them a hiding, they don't—"

"Klaus, stop," said his mother, returning with the broom and dustpan. "This is your father you're talking to."

"Well, who says I even want him for a father?" exploded Klaus, including both his parents in this question. "I have other options now, better ones, things you don't know anything about."

"Oh, really?" said his father, giving a phlegmy chortle. "I suppose you mean the Jesuits and how they're trying to turn you into a priest." The way he said "priest" was the way he would have said "faggot."

Mutter, who had washed the blood off her face while she was gone, gave her son a pitying look. "Don't listen to him, Klaus," she said, putting down her broom and dustpan so she could wrap an arm around his shoulders. "There's nothing wrong with becoming a priest. If God is calling you, you have to answer."

Klaus stood there motionless, flattened by the realization that neither of his parents—not even Mutter—knew the first thing about him. They were as useless as his teachers, he could see that now, and there was no point in expecting anything from them. They were mired in the past—all adults were—and only someone like Uncle Karl was exempt.

Not only did Uncle Karl belong to the future, he actually held it in his hands.

Klaus glanced out the window where a streetlight stood silently, confronting the darkness with its brazen circle of light, and understood what he must do. It might not have been clear before, but now, suddenly, it was.

Times were changing, and he would change with them.

ON SPECIAL ASSIGNMENT:
PARIS 1943

I

When a light tap sounded on the door of Klaus's office (or rather the broom closet he'd been allotted for his visit), he answered with an ill-humored grunt, expecting one of Knochen's minions, come to bother him about some small inconsistency on one of the numerous forms he'd filled out when arriving at headquarters. It was not one of Knochen's men who opened the door, however, but a plump young girl with a delightfully pink complexion. Looking at her, Klaus immediately thought of a Viennese *Knödl*, one of those small sugared dumplings that hide a single ripe strawberry.

"And you are?" he asked, rising and taking the folder she handed him. She must be someone new, he thought, or else he would have remembered her from his last visit to Paris at the end of 1942.

"Olga," she answered, her round face turning an even more vivid shade of pink. "Olga Voss."

"Obersturmführer Klaus Barbie," he replied, clicking his

heels and bowing slightly. She was very nicely formed, he reflected, as curvy and plush as the rolled arm of a sofa and so short that the top of her head barely reached his shoulder. And her mouth was simply adorable, such a dark rosy red and shaped like . . .

She cleared her throat, her face having reddened even more. "Your signature, Herr Obersturmführer," she said, gesturing toward the folder. "It's required."

He opened the folder and saw that it was the forms he himself had filled out on the prisoner he'd delivered earlier in the day. Klaus had no idea who the man was—probably a black marketeer and not much else—but Knochen apparently thought otherwise. "Hands off," he'd warned Klaus over the phone, "and I mean that literally. None of your clumsy techniques."

So, instead of questioning the man in Lyon, which would have been logical, Klaus had been ordered to drive him to avenue Foch. In addition, there were a few other things—odds and ends, Klaus supposed—that Knochen was assigning him. It was exasperating: a section chief from Lyon had better things to do than serve as a lackey for the great Dr. Knochen . . .

Olga coughed lightly. "If I could just have your signature . . ."

Klaus, who had momentarily forgotten her, looked up to see a nervous half-smile on her lips. "Tell you what," he said. "You go to lunch with me, and I'll sign it when we get back. How's that?"

* * *

When they got to the Bouillon Racine a bit later, Klaus was gratified to see Fraulein Voss's small red mouth open into an "O" as she took in the restaurant, which was decorated to look like an Art Nouveau jewelry box. Klaus thought it was ridiculous—all those beveled glass mirrors, the table lamps designed to look like nodding tulips, the long curvaceous bar that was ludicrous in the extreme—but he knew that women were attracted to this kind of excess, that it put them in a receptive mood.

"A table for two," he said to the maître 'd, an anemic-looking man who bowed obsequiously. "Perhaps something with a view."

The maître 'd glanced briefly at Klaus, no doubt taking note of the uniform, then led them to a table near the front window which seemed more for show than actual use. Other diners, watching from the dim recesses at the back of the restaurant, could see them, as could anyone passing on the street. Fraulein Voss seemed embarrassed to be the object of so much scrutiny, but Klaus thoroughly enjoyed their island table. It was almost as if he and Olga were on stage giving a performance of some kind.

"So how long have you been in Paris?" he asked as their consommé arrived.

"Just a few weeks, Herr Obersturmführer," she replied, ducking her head.

"And you're from . . ."

"From Herressen in Thuringia," she said, explaining that her father was a fruit seller there. "A member of the party," she added parenthetically, and Klaus nodded his approval, though it made no difference to him one way or the other. Apparently, things had become unpleasant at home after her mother had died, and so she'd gone to Berlin to take a secretarial training course. Then, after that, she'd applied to the military for a job. "I was lucky to get Paris," she concluded, "because Paris . . . well, everyone wants Paris. It's the City of Light."

Klaus smiled, on the verge of reminding her that nightly

blackouts had all but extinguished those lights, but then he thought better of it: perhaps the city was every bit as bright as she'd expected. In any case, there was no need to say anything since their main course was arriving: *lapin à la moutarde* for him and *boeuf bourguignon* for her.

Olga spent a moment or two studying her plate. "Ach, so good," she said, smiling her thanks before picking up her knife and fork and applying them ardently. It pleased Klaus to see that she was not a dainty eater. So many women only picked at their food, as if it were somehow indecent to reveal any kind of appetite in front of a man. It was refreshing to come across a girl like Olga who dug into her food without dilly-dallying.

While she ate, he told her a little about himself, beginning with his early days on the vice squad in Berlin. He considered this a neutral-enough subject, since women, even women who worked at SD headquarters the way Olga did, could be—well, a little skittish if the conversation strayed too close to the reality of things.

"Berlin was a cesspool in those days," he told her, describing his raids on lurid nightclubs and brothels. "And it was even worse during the Olympics," he added, explaining that they'd been ordered to round up all the prostitutes in the city. "You won't believe it," he said, "but we made them peel potatoes just as they were, in their high heels and feathers and I-don't-know-what-all. It was quite a sight." He laughed loudly at his recollection of the scene, and Olga joined in, giggling into her napkin discreetly.

Then, judging the time was right, he pulled out a photo of little Ute, his daughter, who was back in Trier with her mother. Showing the picture was a ritual of his, a way of making sure that the women he courted knew how things stood with him.

"Wie niedlich," said Olga, who peered at Ute's fat little face and toothless grin, then added in English: "Such a darling."

"You know English?" Klaus asked her, surprised, and she explained that "darling" (more or less the equivalent of *libeling*) was a word she'd picked up while visiting her married sister in London—a sister she hadn't seen in years, not since the war had begun.

"You must miss her," said Klaus politely, his only aim to keep the conversation going.

But Olga responded by prattling on about Hedwig and her family for ten minutes or more. "If I could just send her a letter . . ." she finally said, looking up at Klaus from under her brows.

"A letter?" asked Klaus, who had been only half-listening. "But that's impossible. We're at war with Britain. No contact is allowed."

"I know," said Olga as the crèmes brûlée appeared. "I just thought maybe . . . well, that someone in your position might be able to . . ."

"No, it's impossible. Really, what are you thinking?"

Olga tapped the caramelized top of her custard with the back of her spoon until it splintered. "Of course," she said in a tight, barely audible voice. "I understand there are rules."

Too late Klaus realized his mistake. She was a motherless girl who missed her sister, that's all, so why hadn't he been more tactful, more understanding? Still, he couldn't afford to get caught doing favors, even though he knew it wouldn't be difficult to have Gottlieb mail a letter from Geneva. He was certainly there often enough, either running errands for Klaus or doing a bit of reconnaissance work. The only problem was Olga. She was so silly, so chatty.

Could he trust her to keep her mouth shut?

Snapping his fingers, he summoned the waiter and ordered coffee. Then, leaning across the table, he said, "But perhaps there's something else I can do for you? Perfume maybe or some silk stockings?"

But Olga only shook her head—*no, she didn't need anything like that*—and when the coffee came, she had only one small sip. Klaus was annoyed (there were Parisians who would have traded a week's worth of cigarettes for that coffee), but he tried to ignore her sulking.

"Well, at least let me see you again," he said, looking into her moon-shaped face with its wet red lips. "Some evening this week perhaps?"

Predictably, though, she prevaricated: *Well, not that night, but perhaps the next. She would have to see. But she had enjoyed lunch, please don't think that she hadn't, it had been a real treat.* This was not what Klaus wanted to hear, but he took it for what it was: a feeble attempt to preserve her dignity.

"I understand," he said amiably enough as the bill was presented on a small silver tray. "But remember, I could be called back to Lyon at any moment."

II

Meanwhile, Josephine Butler, who was approaching Le Fouquet's on the Champs Élyseés, felt a fist tighten around her heart. Was this a café, she wondered, or a Germans-only canteen? But there was no turning back now. She'd been commissioned to track the comings and goings of Admiral Canaris, so if Le Fouquet's was the place he frequented, she had no choice but to install herself there.

Quickly, she scanned the outdoor tables, taking in the blur of uniforms: the Wehrmacht in grayish-green, the Luftwaffe in blue, and—worst of all, lounging front and center—a trio of Gestapo men dressed sleekly in black. Sitting there, with their long legs sprawled out in front of them, drinking coffee and cognac and smoking what was almost certainly real tobacco, they looked a little ridiculous, like fourteen-year-old boys who'd raided an uncle's liquor cabinet. But Josephine knew they were anything but harmless—and so, apparently, did everyone else, judging by the empty tables surrounding them.

For a moment, she stood there pondering—*weren't there any other seats anywhere?* — but then, realizing that she was standing there like a ninny, she made herself choose one of the empty tables and started walking toward it. *Be decisive, that's the important thing,* she told herself, sitting down as casually as she could and looking around with what she hoped was a bored expression. The SS men, a table or two to her left, had barely looked up as she passed, which was good, just what she wanted. Not only that, but the table she'd chosen gave her an unobstructed view of the boulevard.

She signaled the waiter and ordered a *café noir*, or whatever it was they were calling coffee these days and took a deep breath to calm herself. Waiting in cafés was part of her job, but it was always nerve-wracking. Conjuring up her younger self—

the *jeune fille* who had left England to study in Paris—was one of her tricks. That girl, as she recalled, had spent a lot of time waiting for *beaux* in places not so different from this one.

She was no longer young, of course, but the way you looked (the color of your hair or the shape of your face or the makeup you were wearing) didn't matter as much as the story you projected.

Cover, the SOE called it.

In her pre-war life, Josephine had been a physician with a busy practice in London. It was what she had always intended to do. While other little girls played elaborate games with their dolls, dressing them up like brides or treating them like babies, Josephine wrapped hers in bandages or subjected them to injections administered with a hatpin. The notion that she would ever do anything except practice medicine had never crossed her mind. But then, quite without warning, she'd been summoned for service abroad, something very hush-hush that Churchill himself had dreamed up. Josephine supposed that someone must have recommended her for the job, though who that person might have been she couldn't imagine. There must have been a vetting process as well. At any rate, the officer who interviewed her on Baker Street had been very well-informed, knowing without Josephine's telling him that she'd studied at the Sorbonne, that her French was excellent—and that she wasn't married. In addition, her parents were dead (the officer seemed quite cheerful about this), meaning that, as he put it, she had no obligations of a personal nature. Surely, he concluded, it would be no problem for her to suspend her practice, just for the duration, while she undertook some special assignments.

Her decision to do so had eventually led Josephine here, to this outdoor café where she was hoping to spot Admiral Canaris, a man who was known to disapprove of Hitler.

Josephine had no idea if he might go so far as to try to over-throw the Führer, but that was obviously Churchill's hope.

A white-aproned waiter appeared just then with her coffee, and Josephine forced herself to take a small sip. It was bitter, barely drinkable, like water out of a rusty drainpipe, but it was all you could get after three years of German occupation. She'd heard it was made from roasted barley, but she would have believed anything: bark, wood shavings, even mouse droppings.

Ersatz, that was the German word for it, and it applied to practically everything these days. Shoes weren't soled in leather anymore, but in wood. Cigarettes weren't made from tobacco, but from sunflower leaves or some other "approximation." Even Josephine herself was ersatz, a Parisienne only by virtue of the small chic hat and warm French coat she wore. She'd found them at a second-hand shop on rue Rocher, where they were expensive but not as expensive as they looked. Besides, a good coat wasn't an extravagance, it was camouflage.

Josephine's drama teacher at St. Swithin's had taught her the usefulness of costumes. Put on Lady Macbeth's nightgown, dip your hands in raspberry jam and, voilà! You *are* Lady Macbeth. It was risky, though: Play the role enough times and you could lose track of yourself. That was why, underneath her fancy French clothes, Josephine still wore British-made under-wear: a Marks & Spencer brassiere and sensible cotton knick-ers, both rather the worse for wear, but still holding up, thank goodness.

She sipped her coffee and stared intently at the boulevard for a few minutes before reminding herself that the SS were only three or four yards away. So far, they'd paid no attention to her, but if she looked too anxious, they might. Perhaps it was time for *Je suis partout*, she thought, pulling that week's edition out of her bag and shaking it open with a flourish. It was a scur-rilous rag, but a very useful prop if you were forced to share space with Nazis. She spread it out on the marble-topped table in front of her and started turning the pages, searching for an article that was halfway readable. *Just pick one, it doesn't matter,* she told herself, finally settling on a long article about the French aircraft industry and how it was busy churning out planes for the Luftwaffe. When she'd read it twice and then summarized it to herself, just as a mental exercise, she looked up again hoping to catch sight of Canaris, but all she saw was a dilapidated old man, some sixty yards off, wobbling alongside the gutter.

She returned to her paper, turning over to the next page where a photo showed Ambassador Abetz welcoming someone or other to the German Institute. She had just started in on the accompanying article when she happened to overhear fragments of conversation coming from the Gestapo table.

"Nicely turned out, but a bit past her prime, wouldn't you say?" joked one of them, glancing in Josephine's direction. He was big and aggressively blond, a propaganda poster come to life.

"Oh, I don't know," answered one of the other two. "Women her age, they're a gift. Grateful for any attention you give them." He picked his teeth idly. "It makes them more tractable."

A general guffaw followed, and Josephine felt her cheeks growing warm. She fought back the urge to throw them a scorching look. But to do so would have been an admission that she understood German.

Then the third officer weighed in. He was sallow-faced and had a long nose, rather like a ferret's. "You're pathetic," he told his companions in a Berlin drawl, giving Josephine a quick glance. "You'd be lucky to get the time of day out of that *gnädige Frau.*" He fished a handkerchief from his back pocket and blew his nose with a loud honk, then summoned a nearby waiter with a snap of his fingers.

"*Oui, messieurs soldats,*" said the waiter, a thin, stooped man who nodded attentively as he took their order, then hurried away to get their bottle of cognac. When he returned, he topped off their cups of coffee, turning the mouth of the bottle at just the right moment to keep it from dripping. But then the blond one bumped the waiter's forearm—Josephine was quite sure it had been deliberate—and a little of the cognac dribbled onto the black sleeve of his tunic.

"Watch what you're doing, old man," said Propaganda Boy, holding out his arm and shaking it menacingly, pretending that his sleeve had been drenched.

The waiter, with the solid dignity of his profession, bowed slightly and murmured an apology. But then, walking away, he tripped on something (his long apron? a jack-booted foot?) and the metal tray he'd been holding clattered to the pavement. The sound, exploding behind Josephine like the report of a pistol, was so sudden and sharp she couldn't help jumping as the tray rolled away, veering this way and that before hitting the leg of a table and toppling over with a clang.

Wrong! don't make yourself conspicuous, she told herself. But hadn't everyone else jumped too? It would have been suspicious if she'd remained unnaturally calm.

She fingered the small gold cross at her throat and looked out over the boulevard where she saw the old man still picking his way toward the café. Unsteady on his feet and coughing loudly, he jerked his way along like a rag doll or a puppet, his eyes fixed on the gutter. From time to time, he bent over, plucked a cigarette butt from the pavement, then wavered up again, holding his small treasure at arm's length for a moment before tucking it into a saggy pants pocket.

Josephine was not without sympathy. After all, who knew

what his troubles were. Chronic bronchitis? Tuberculosis? Or perhaps he'd been gassed in the last war, so many had been. Still, she couldn't help feeling upset. To be old and sick was no crime, but to parade your misery up and down the Champs Élysées where every off-duty Boche could take in the spectacle was demeaning and shameful.

A few more patrons trickled into the café and Josephine took a quick inventory. A woman in a red hat with a small, vicious-looking dog on her lap. An elfin man whose pipe and pointed goatee made him look like a professor. And there, in the corner, a heedless young couple who couldn't stop touching.

Meanwhile, the puppet-man edged closer. The bottom half of his face looked shrunken, as if his back teeth were missing, and even though it was cold—quite cold—he had no coat: only a worn-out suit jacket and a sad scrap of scarf that might have been blue or green once but was now the dead color of cement.

Seeing him, the SS men laughed hugely: what fun, this *besoffen* old bum shambling along, oblivious of everything except his precious tobacco. They tossed a couple of half-smoked cigarettes in his direction, cheering derisively as he scooped them up. But instead of being scornful, or at least embarrassed, as Josephine would have hoped, he stood there grinning like a clown, smiling his gap-toothed smile and touching a palsied hand to the brim of his cap.

A nervous hush settled over the café. Conversation slowed, eyes were averted. Even the young lovers looked uncomfortable.

"God, what a useless old bastard," said one of the SS men, looking around the café belligerently. "Fritz, promise you'll shoot me if I ever get that old." Then guffaws erupted again as one of them—it was the ferret-faced one—tossed another cigarette butt in the direction of the old man, who immediately pounced on it. It was then, before anyone could realize what was happening—before the recipient even had a chance to straighten up—that the blond-headed officer was out of his seat and standing over him with the heel of his boot held flat against the old man's neck. He squirmed, trying to free himself, but then, within seconds, he was still. He's blacked out, that's all, Josephine told herself, hopeful when the jack-boot was finally lifted and the old man managed to lift his head a little way off the sidewalk. It lolled like a freshly born kitten's, but, yes, he was alive. Surely, they'd leave him alone now. But then the boot slammed down again, this time with even greater force, while its wearer surveyed the crowd around him with disinterest, as if he had no idea what his foot was doing. Then finally, as if recalling, he looked down, saw the *Untermensch* and lifted his foot from the man's neck. The movement was as smooth and impersonal as if he'd released the clutch while driving. Then fastidiously, as if to avoid contact, he turned the body over with the toe of his boot and nudged it gently to see—or rather to show—that the body was lifeless.

A dome of silence descended over the *café-terrasse* and in that silence fingers were snapped, the headwaiter summoned. "Here, take him away," ordered the man who had done the killing.

Josephine plunged her hands into her lap to hide their shaking as the corpse was removed. Every atom in her body strained to escape—if only she could leave, simply pick up her things and get out of here—but how could she when her job was to stay and watch for Canaris? She looked around cautiously, just in case she might have missed him, then nearly gasped when she spotted a cripple crutching his way along the same gutter, once again searching for German cigarettes. *No,* she wanted to shout: *Don't do that, go somewhere else, it's not safe, they'll kill you.* But the words were only in her head where the cripple couldn't hear them. He had no idea what had happened here only ten minutes before.

Once again, the café held its breath, waiting, watching for the inevitable cigarette to come flying through the air. Josephine didn't see the SS man who threw it, but his aim was poor and the cigarette rolled in the direction of her table. Without thinking, almost without knowing, she reached out with her foot and stamped on it, grinding it into the cobblestones as though it were something lethal, an ampoule of anthrax spores or a tarantula poised to sting.

Finally, having destroyed it, she sat back in her rattan chair, aware, suddenly, that everyone was staring at her, their mouths slack with horror. Then she heard a chair scraping against the sidewalk and realized that she had broken the cardinal rule: she had made herself conspicuous. Even without looking, she could sense one of the black-suited men approaching.

III

When they brought her to him, Klaus was impressed. She wasn't young—probably in her forties—but he saw at once that she had class. Her coat was well made—expensive—and she was wearing a fetching little hat with a veil that seemed to magnify her blue eyes. In addition, she had a delicately moist complexion (rare except among English women) and, though she wasn't particularly tall, she stood erect.

He listened to what the men from the café had to say, then scanned her papers (Solange Préjean, a schoolteacher from Eure et Loire, etc.). He positioned himself in front of the window and looked directly at her. "Why do you dislike Germans?" he asked quietly in French.

"I did not say I disliked Germans," Jospehine replied, glancing at her inquisitor, noting the Iron Cross on his left breast pocket, the collar tabs that indicated the rank of Obersturmführer. So, a lieutenant, that was all. Still, he was young (in his twenties probably) so Obersturmführer was no doubt an accomplishment. Nor was he bad looking, in fact rather handsome.

"I'm sorry I acted the way I did," she continued. "It was on the spur of the moment." She paused, praying that something plausible would come to her, then added: "You see, I am a schoolteacher and therefore very fond of children, and I have always felt—well, perhaps it sounds silly—but I have always felt that elderly people are rather like children. They need protecting."

The Obersturmführer looked at her with his large pale eyes—either blue or gray, she wasn't sure—and frowned slightly.

"I am inclined to believe that you are more of an aristocrat than a teacher," he said, and Josephine felt her stomach shrivel.

Perhaps the stylish coat and hat had been a mistake. A school-teacher wasn't likely to own such fine things.

"You are certainly very cool and collected," he continued. "Where do you teach?"

Josephine had her lines prepared: she was a relief teacher currently between posts. She was now waiting to be reassigned.

Klaus nodded. It was a dull story, so dull it was probably true. But he wasn't sure. Her self-possession spoke against it. Most women, when they were hauled into Gestapo headquarters, were jumpy and tense. Bark at them and they'd start to cry. But Mlle Préjean seemed immune to her surroundings. She could just as easily have been in the lobby of a theater or on the corner of a busy street. He decided to test her.

"Strip," he ordered, keeping his voice quiet.

Josephine was stunned. Surely, she had misunderstood. "Do you mean remove all my clothes?" she asked, her throat dry.

"Yes, and hurry up," he snapped. "Or would you like some help?"

There were snickers from the Gestapo men standing around, the three who had brought her in plus a couple of others who had wandered in, and for a moment Josephine was afraid her knees would buckle. She glanced around the small office, at the filing cabinet, the calendar on the wall, anywhere but at their faces, and reached for her hat. Fumbling for her hatpin with stiff, clumsy fingers, she recalled her arthritic patients and how the simplest things were monumental tasks for them. Now she knew what that felt like. Finally, though, she found the head of the hatpin and managed to extract it.

She lifted the little dome of black velvet from her head and wondered what she was supposed to do with it. She looked around, uncertain, until the Obersturmführer pointed to the center of his desk.

She laid the hat down carefully, almost like a sacrifice, and began on her gloves. They were kidskin, a tight fit even under ordinary circumstances. She tugged at the fingertips, but the gloves seemed to have shrunk to her hands, almost like a new layer of skin. She glanced at her interrogator, hoping for what— a reprieve?—but he stood motionless, his face frozen over. Finally, not knowing what else to do, she resorted to biting the tips of the fingers and yanking the gloves off with her teeth.

Klaus watched with interest. Her teeth were small and white and seeing her use them in this unexpected way was a revelation. Perhaps, he thought, there was a *bête sauvage* hidden inside every woman.

Josephine laid the gloves on the desk beside her hat and felt for the buttons on her coat. As if in a trance she began to undo them, her hands performing the task without direction from her brain. Through the open door of the office, she heard secretaries clacking away on typewriters or speaking into their phones. How nice it would be to be one of those women, she thought: typing things up, answering the phone, alphabetizing files—such an easy and comfortable job, no risk of any kind, just go home at the end of—

"Come on, hurry up," goaded one of the men standing nearby, and Josephine, startled, glanced down to see her coat hanging open. Strange, because she didn't remember undoing the buttons, yet obviously she had. Once more she scanned the room, looking for a place to put her coat, but the office seemed to have been stripped of anything remotely suggesting hospitality— no chairs, not so much as a hook on the back of the door. Nor was the Obersturmführer offering up any more space on his desk. She looked down at the parquet flooring—once elegant, now stained and dirty—and shrugged off her coat, letting it fall to the floor in a heap, its pale mauve lining sadly exposed.

Now only her skirt and blouse were left, that was all. And once they were removed, she'd be standing there in her slip, wearing less than she did when she went to bed. It was hot in the office—stiflingly so—yet she couldn't help shivering.

Klaus took note of the shivering (a point in her favor) and admitted that he was enjoying himself. Watching a woman undressing slowly never failed to thrill him. The stage version, a stripper performing for an audience, was always a cheat: even as you sat there, titillated, watching as layer after layer dropped away, you knew she was never going to give up everything. Some small shreds of cloth would cling to her even at the end of the act, depriving you of the all-inclusive vision you craved. But in real life it was different. So far Mlle Préjean had managed to maintain her poise. Well, good for her. But from here on out it wouldn't be so easy. With each item of clothing she was forced to relinquish, she'd be losing a little more of her self-possession.

Josephine fingered the buttons on her blouse—tiny dome-shaped buttons, a long row of them, covered to match the crêpe de chine of the blouse—and began undoing them as slowly as she dared. The first two were easy, but from the third one on down, she knew that the top of her slip would be revealed. That was bad enough, but infinitely worse was the telltale brassiere just underneath. She cursed herself for being so stupid. Hadn't she heard of agents who would have passed had it not been for the label in their underwear? Her mother had always warned her about being overly confident, that it would get her in trouble someday if she didn't watch out, and now that day was here.

Across from her, Klaus watched intently as Mlle Préjean untucked her blouse from the band of her skirt, pulled her arms free of the sleeves and tossed the blouse on top of her coat. A moment ago, he would have said that her elegance came from her clothes, but now, gazing at her, he realized it was actually the reverse. Indeed, every part of her was imbued with elegance. The slenderness of her arms. The length of her neck. The neatness of her breasts, which were as high and dainty as a girl's. He might have preferred breasts that were a bit larger, but it hardly mattered, he was aroused all the same.

Josephine, reaching behind her to undo her skirt, caught the flicker of lust in his eyes but pushed it away. She had to. Panic was pressing in on her from every direction, and anything else, anything at all, might break her. It would be so easy just to give way to the fear and collapse in a heap on top of her clothes. That was probably what they wanted. But they'd had their fun with the old man, that was enough. *Lord, help me*, she prayed silently, staring at her hat and gloves in the middle of the Obersturmführer's desk and concentrating all of her energy on the hook and eye at the back of her skirt. But it wouldn't budge, or rather her fingers couldn't manage the task.

Klaus saw the trouble she was having and nearly stepped forward to assist her before remembering that this was not a domestic scene. Still, he couldn't help imagining his hand pulling down the tab of her zipper and then drifting slowly, so slowly if might have been an accident, across the curve of her rump. And if he did that, what would she do? Cringe? Burst into tears? Start wailing? It would be interesting to see.

But finally Josephine, using her nails, was able to pry the tiny hook away from its even tinier eye. She undid the zipper, easy by comparison, and her skirt dropped to the floor. She stepped out of it lightly, then pushed it out of the way with her foot, noticing a dark stain near one of the desk legs that reminded her of a Rorschach print. Impassively, she wondered if it might be a bloodstain.

"Get on with it," said the Obersturmführer. "This shouldn't take all day."

Josephine, her heart pounding inside its basket of ribs,

fingered one strap of her slip, wishing she could think of some way to stall. If it had been an interrogation, she might have been able to talk her way out of it. But this, she thought, pushing one strap off her shoulder, was an altogether different interrogation—an interrogation without words.

"C'mon, c'mon," said one of the others, a blotchy-faced NCO who looked as if he drank. "The other one too."

Reluctantly, Josephine pushed the other strap off her shoulder, and it was then, just as the top of the slip sagged to reveal the alien bra underneath, that she caught the Obersturmführer in a leer—a leer so fat and greasy, so unmistakably obvious (he wasn't even trying to hide it) that this time there was no way of shoving it aside. She felt a thickness in her throat, a sudden wave of wooziness. *Please, God,* she prayed, touching the cross at her neck, *please save me from this ordeal.*

Slowly, as if guided by a force outside herself, she lifted her head and brought her eyes up to meet his. There is goodness in everyone, even in one of Hitler's *borreaux,* she told herself, looking directly at him and searching his pale eyes for some hint of mercy.

Klaus, surprised by the audacity of her gaze, was taken aback. Prisoners did not generally look him in the eye (or, if they did, it was only because they were practiced liars), yet here she was, petitioning him with a gaze so direct it felt almost intimate. During his training, he'd been told that no one, not even the weakest prisoner, was without power. Chained or beaten, it made no difference, they were still quite capable of pressing their advantage. He'd never given the notion much credence, but perhaps there was some truth in it. Before he could pursue his thoughts much further, though, a faint noise in the hallway —an intake of breath or a small exclamation—distracted him.

It was Olga, standing just inside the doorway, staring at

Mlle Préjean in horror. It was as if the floor in front of her had suddenly opened up to reveal a pit full of rats.

Klaus was mystified. A woman in her underwear, what was so shocking about that?

But then Olga lifted her eyes to his, and her gaze, though searching and dispassionate at first, quickly hardened into something mask-like. "Sorry," she murmured. "I didn't know." And then, as quickly as she'd appeared, she was gone.

Well, good riddance, thought Klaus. A little goose whose only talent was giggling—who cared? Had she no idea what went on in SD headquarters? What she had seen was nothing. Nothing! If she wanted, he could show her something much worse, something more in keeping with her misplaced pity.

He stepped away from the window and glanced at the men loitering around his office.

"This is a waste of time," he barked. Then, turning to Mlle Préjean, he said, "You may dress." He waved the others away as if they were flies and then sat down at his desk, took out a file and started to make notations in it.

Josephine, stunned, pulled on her clothes as quickly as she could, afraid that at any moment he might change his mind. All she could think of was getting away from this awful, airless building and out onto the street where the crowds would cover her up. But then, just as she was about to pick up her hat and gloves, the Obersturmführer stopped her.

"Leave those," he commanded. "I am inclined to believe you, but you are not going yet."

IV

It was a couple of days later, after Klaus had finally lured Olga into his bed (all it had taken was a promise to mail her letter, such a small thing really) that she asked him about the woman she'd seen in his office.

"What woman?" he asked, watching as the smoke from his cigarette drifted lazily toward the ceiling.

"You know, the one you made strip in front of everybody."

Klaus frowned. "Well, you can hardly call it stripping when all she took off was the outer layer."

"Oh, I thought you made her take off everything."

"No, there was no need," said Klaus, tapping the ashes from his cigarette into the ashtray that was balanced on his belly. "She was just a hapless schoolteacher. In the wrong place at the wrong time, that's all."

"So what did you do to her?"

"Oh, nothing much. I gave her two days' hard labor, that's all."

"Hard labor?"

"Oh, it wasn't so bad," he said. "Scrubbing floors, cleaning boots, that sort of thing. She got off easy."

Olga was quiet for a moment. "But do you think she was really a schoolteacher?"

"Why, don't you?"

"No, not really," she said, rolling over onto her side so that her magnificent *Busen* was on full display. "To tell you the truth," she added, "I'm not even sure she was French."

"So, after only a few weeks in Paris," said Klaus, teasing her gently, "you can tell who's French and who isn't?"

"Well, no, not exactly, but in this case . . . well, didn't you wonder about her brassiere?"

"Her brassiere?" asked Klaus.

"I know it sounds silly," she said quickly, "but I recognized it right away. It was just like Hedwig's."

Klaus looked at her in bewilderment.

"Hedwig, my sister in London," she said. "You're mailing my letter to her."

"Oh, right," he said, blowing out a series of smoke rings that floated up to the ceiling.

"Anyway," she continued, "the thing about Hedwig is that she buys all her brassieres from Marks and Sparks and—"

"Marks and Sparks?"

"It's really Marks & Spencer—people just call it Marks and Sparks—but the interesting thing about them is that everything they sell is British-made. It's what sets them apart from other department stores."

Klaus had been only half-listening, but the term "British-made" jumped out at him.

"What exactly are you saying, Olga?" he asked.

"Well, I'm not sure. It just seems strange that she'd be wearing a brassiere you could get only in Britain, that's all."

Klaus stubbed out his half-smoked cigarette and set the ashtray down on the floor. He knew the routine well enough, how you needed to check hat bands and labels—well, everything really—but it hadn't occurred to him that it was necessary in the case of Mlle Préjean. She simply hadn't *seemed* like an operative. If he'd been wrong, though, and she were brought in again—this time on something more substantial than crushing a cigarette under the sole of her shoe—he'd have to pray that Knochen never found out that he'd been the one who released her. Knochen had never much liked him anyway, and Klaus knew he'd be only too happy to cut him loose. Isn't that what had happened to Dannecker, sent away to Bulgaria? And Heinrichsohn too: he'd been a Jew-lover of course, but marching him off to the Eastern front? It would have been easier just to put a noose around his neck and be done with it.

"But she could have gotten the brassiere as a gift," said Klaus, turning onto his side to face Olga. "Or maybe she went to London for a vacation and bought it then. You don't know. There could be a hundred explanations."

Olga brushed aside his protests. "Maybe, but didn't you notice how shabby and worn-out it was? Everything else of hers was so elegant—the coat, the hat, that crêpe de chine—"

"But if she'd been trained by the SOE," Klaus cut in, "don't you think she would have been more careful? She would have known better than to wear something that could give her away."

Olga considered this. "Yes, you'd think so," she said. "But people are funny. They turn all sorts of things into good-luck charms."

"That's what you think it was? A good-luck charm?"

"Well, maybe," said Olga. "Either that, or a reminder of home." She paused for a moment, then added, "You never know, wearing it might have given her a bit of courage." She said this in such a wistful way that it seemed as if she knew Mlle Préjean personally.

"Listen, Olga," said Klaus, propping himself up on his elbow, "you've got to promise me that you'll be careful not to mention this to anyone else, especially not in the office."

Olga's eyes shone. "So you think she was a spy? Is that what you're saying?"

"No. No, of course not, but this whole thing . . . well, it's somewhat irregular. I mean, it might be a bit difficult to . . ."

"A bit difficult to explain?"

"Yes, something like that," he said, stung by the jaunty, almost taunting tone of her voice. He tried out a small smile on her and waited for her to smile back, or perhaps even giggle (wasn't she a champion giggler?), but Olga only looked at him blankly.

"Well, I wouldn't worry," she finally said, a little light of contempt coming into her eyes as she studied him. "Whoever she was, she's long gone now."

Klaus didn't know what to say to this, but there was no need to say anything. Olga, apparently done with him, was busy fluffing her pillow. Then, turning her back to him, she lay down and glided off to sleep as effortlessly as a child. For Klaus it was different, though. He lay awake for hours, smoking one cigarette after another and staring at the expanse of white ceiling above him. Russia was like that, he thought, just an endless stretch of snow and ice that reduced humans to ants. He could see himself there, gnawing on a frozen mule shank and watching while his toes turned black from frostbite.

But he was being irrational. Insomnia always did that to him. Still, there was no getting around the fact that he'd been sloppy—and sloppiness was not something the SD overlooked.

Just ask Dannecker or Heinrichsohn.

He sat up then and, looking over at Olga, cursed her under his breath. What had she thought she was doing anyway, barging into his office the way she had? Hadn't she known that an interrogation was underway? And why seize on some small inconsistency (maybe useful, maybe not) only to harbor it until —voilà!—she could hurl it back at him like a grenade?

He had let a viper into his bed, he realized, gazing down at the sweat-dampened curls that were stuck to the nape of her neck. Mindlessly, he reached out and touched one of them with his forefinger, noticing at the same time how thin her neck was. To measure, he dropped his hand onto the back of her neck, his thumb on one side, fingers on the other. Beneath the palm of his hand, he could feel the knob of a vertebra. There were seven in the neck, stacked up like shelves, and quite delicate really, more delicate than people realized . . . But then, with a sudden jerk, he snatched his hand away. This was craziness. What was he thinking? She was a little girl, a goose.

Only hours before, he'd been cooing in her ear. And he was unhinged enough now to think . . . Quickly, he threw himself onto his side of the bed and lay there as if pinned to the mattress, waiting for his chest to stop banging. People talked about men, SD men like himself, who'd gone off the rails and lost their effectiveness. This had been a close call, no question about it, but he'd be careful in the future, he'd keep himself in check. Because he couldn't afford to let this war weaken him.

Others might crumble, but not him, not Klaus Barbie.

NUMBER 12 RUE SAINTE-CATHERINE

Early on February 9, 1943

The weather is cold and sleety when André Deutsch picks up his briefcase full of cash and heads for the UGIF office at eight-thirty in the morning. Mondays are always a trial for him. On those days (allotment days) he has to lug as much as 30,000 francs through Old Lyon with its medieval lanes and narrow soot-stained buildings. André has never been especially brave, (he was a *yeshiva* boy, an easy target for the roughnecks in his town of Borsec) but walking alone through this part of the city would make anyone jumpy. Just thinking about the extensive network of underground *traboules* and who might be hiding in them is enough to make his stomach contract, his bowels loosen. How much easier things would be if the deliveries could be made in a normal way (by armored car, say), but there is nothing normal about the Union Générale des Israelites de France. How could there be when the UGIF was cooked up by the SS in collusion with the Vichy government? Still, it's the only social service agency the Jews have in France. And André knows that he's lucky to work there as an accountant. He just wishes the job didn't entail carrying a bagful of cash through a city teeming with refugees, some so desperate they'd probably kill for a ration card.

Fortunately, though, this will be the last delivery he'll ever have to make since he'll be relocating to Savoie next week. The Italians are in charge there, and they don't really care who's Jewish and who isn't, or at least that's what he's been told.

But in the meantime, he has a long walk ahead of him and he's scared. Anyone who's ever come into the office looking for a handout would be able to recognize him—and guess what was in the briefcase. André doesn't know what he'd do if he was accosted. But obviously he'd have to do something because in 1943 a Romanian Jew in France is on his own. Call for the police and you're likely to find yourself in the lap of the Gestapo.

* * *

Meanwhile, Maier Weissman is at home packing his rucksack with toys for the children. His staff tells him to focus on useful things—shoes, toothbrushes, flannel underwear, that sort of thing—and he agrees, it's UGIF's job to provide those things, but he also knows that games and dolls and comic books are just as important—perhaps, in a way, even more so.

He squeezes in one last teddy bear, then turns to say goodbye to his family: a quick kiss for Miriam, his wife, a hug for Sylvie, his married (or if her husband is dead, widowed) daughter, and finally a big sloppy smooch for Ezekiel, his five-month-old grandson. "Don't worry if I'm a bit late tonight," he tells them. "Monday, you know." Then pausing just long enough to give his wife a mischievous look, he adds, "But I'll be back to help you blow out the candles."

Miriam's look passes from him to Sylvie. "What's this about candles?"

Maier laughs. "For your cake, Miriam. Your birthday cake. You are having a birthday, aren't you?"

"Yes, but—"

"Never you mind," says Maier, winking at his daughter. "Sylvie has it well in hand."

It's how he tries to leave them, on a cheerful note, always with some small reference to the evening ahead. But no sooner is he in the hall, pulling the door shut behind him than a momentary fear washes over him: *What if I don't return? What if I never see them again?* The feeling passes, but not before he's put a hand to his heart—yes, that's what it feels like, a heart attack—and never without a last wistful look at the door, behind which his family is already starting to do whatever it is they do when he's not with them.

*　*　*

At the same time, in a small apartment on rue Vendome, twenty-year-old Eva Gottlieb is sipping a mug of ersatz coffee when her mother appears in the kitchen bundled up like a kulak. Eva takes one look at her—from the Russian-style scarf on her head to the oversized galoshes on her feet—and bursts out laughing. "Oh, *maman*," she says, "you look like a babushka."

Her mother frowns. "Have you glanced out the window, *ma chère*? Don't you see that it's snowing?" But then she glances at the ridiculous galoshes, which were once her son's, and laughs herself. "I just hope I make it to work and back," she says.

Eva takes another sip of her coffee. "Lucky for me I get to

stay in," she says, grateful to have the day off after her eighty-mile trip back from the Swiss border yesterday.

But her mother only looks at her. "Eva, you're not going to miss your piano lesson, are you?"

"My piano lesson?"

"Yes, your piano lesson. It's at nine o'clock on Mondays, isn't it?"

"Today is Monday?"

"*Oui, c'est aujourd'hui lundi,*" says her mother, who starts wrapping up a little bread and some cheese for her lunch. "And Mme Larcher needs every *sou* she can scrape together. Besides," she adds, "you know how much you love to play. It's your passion."

Eva smiles. It's ridiculous, but her mother still believes that she was born with an extravagant gift for music, that if it hadn't been for the war she'd be a concert pianist by now. Eva knows better—she is competent at best—and, besides, the real reason for keeping up with her lessons is to maintain contact with Jacques, Mme Larcher's twenty-two-year-old son. As a courier for Combat, he spends his days cycling from one rendezvous to the next, delivering mail and wireless crystals, sometimes even pistols or cash. Eva never knows where he will be, but he drops by his mother's apartment from time to time to leave her notes. Sometimes it's only a *"Je t'adore"* or a *"Je t'embrasse,"* but if his cousin's flat is available (as it often is since he's a traveling salesman) then Jacques will tell her what time to meet him there.

Eva's life is so chaotic she tries never to think too far ahead, but the possibility of a night together—a whole night, just the two of them, in the same bed like a married couple—is too delirium-inducing to resist. So even without her mother's coaxing, she probably would have devised a way to get to Mme Larcher's today. Still, it's best if she goes at the time of her lesson since showing up at any other time might seem suspicious.

"All right, *maman*," she says, "I'll go, and on my way back I'll stop at UGIF to see if I can give you a hand." Eva's mother is the *secrétaire générale* for one of the departments there, and Eva, who has the nominal title of assistant typist, feels compelled to drop by occasionally just to protect her cover.

"Besides," she adds, "I need to see M. Weissman about our next 'shipment.'"

* * *

Not far off, in a luxury hotel requisitioned by the SD, Obersturmführer Klaus Barbie is briefing the half dozen men gathered in his office. In less than an hour, they'll be setting up a *sourcière* on rue Sainte-Catherine—a mousetrap, that is, with everything as usual out on the street and none of their victims knowing anything about it until they actually walk through the door. It's the strategy Klaus prefers for congested areas like Old Lyon, and he doesn't foresee any problems. His men, with one exception, are all from Section IV, so they'll know what to do. And Stengritt, who's the exception, is in another category altogether since Klaus is bringing him along as an assistant and personal bodyguard. Klaus doubts he'll need a bodyguard—an operation like this, it should be child's play—but he knows he can trust Stengritt. He's solid and steady, the exact opposite of somebody like Koth who gets his jollies from playing the heavy.

When Klaus comes to the end of his briefing, he looks at the men ranged in front of him, letting his gaze rest on each of them in turn. "Any questions?" he asks. There's a brief pause while he waits, but no one says anything. "All right, then," he says, consulting his watch, "get yourselves ready. We leave in thirty minutes."

Klaus waits until his men have filed out before pulling open a desk drawer and getting out his own weapon, a 9mm American pistol. He drops it into the holster fastened on the right side of his belt and glances at himself in the mirror beside his desk. The hôtel Terminus de Perrache specializes in mirrors (fancy wallpaper and sculpted wood paneling, too), all of which Klaus considers rather decadent, effeminate actually, yet here he is, gazing at himself the same way a woman would. He frowns at his reflection, unhappy that the weight of the pistol makes his belt droop, which in turn spoils the lines of his new suit, a navy wool gabardine with the thinnest of pinstripes.

It had been made by a tailor he'd found in the back room of a dry goods store: a Pole (quite likely a Jew as well), but what does he care when the man is a genius with needle and thread? Klaus turns one way and then the other, admiring the fit of his new suit: the sleeves just the right length, the collar matching the curve of his neck exactly. He was lucky to have found someone so talented. Just putting on one of this man's suits makes him look taller—or perhaps not taller exactly, since Klaus knows he'll always look stunted next to a lanky good-looking guy like Stengritt—yet there is something about a suit with this kind of elegance that speaks for itself. Without any designation of rank, it announces to everyone that he is *der chef*.

9 o'clock in the morning

By the time Eva Gottlieb arrives at Mme Larcher's, she's a mess. Her hair is damp and stringy, and her shoes are so wet they squish when she walks. But Mme Larcher, as elegant and composed as ever, seems oblivious.

"*Entrez,*" she says, ushering her pupil into a drawing room that is disconcertingly blank.

Two years ago when Eva first started her lessons, there were paintings in heavy gold frames (originals, she thought) and delicate pieces of Limoges. Now all of those things have been sold, as well as the rugs and most of the chairs, leaving nothing of value except Mme Larcher's grand piano. It stands near the window, glossy and black, its top lifted in a one-winged salute.

"I'm sorry I'm so wet, but it's a nasty day," says Eva, folding her umbrella and propping it in a corner.

Mme Larcher clucks sympathetically. "You are so right, my dear. But what can we do?" She helps Eva out of her coat and hangs it on a hook. "The important thing is that you're here. So many of my students have . . ." Her voice trails off, probably out of delicacy (a lady does not mention her poverty), but Eva knows how circumscribed her life has become. The bare room speaks for itself.

Hoping to change the subject, Eva pulls some sheet music out of her bag. "Look," she says, "a friend from work let me borrow these Beethoven pieces. I thought maybe you could help me with them."

Mme Larcher laughs good-naturedly. "*You* are ready for Beethoven?" she asks, but then adds in a more serious tone of voice, "*Mais pourquois pas?* In times like these, we need Beethoven more than ever."

As Mme Larcher leads the way to her piano, Eva wonders about Jacques. *Isn't there a note from him?* But Madame has said nothing, so she has to assume that there isn't.

Eva arranges herself on the bench, then spreads out her music on the rack. As always, she's a little intimidated by this piano of Mme Larcher's, which is not just a piano but a Blüthner, a make so renowned that it was the choice (as Madame often points out) of Liszt and Tchaikovsky. Even the last tsar had one.

Eva's playing is in sad contrast to this magnificent instrument, but she can't help feeling excited as she sits in front of it. This is Beethoven after all! She straightens her back and takes a deep breath, ready to let her fingers drop onto the keys when Mme Larcher interrupts her.

"Oh, before we start, I should give you this," she says, reaching inside the jet-beaded sleeve of her dress and extracting a small piece of paper that's been folded so many times it's hardly larger than a ration stamp.

Eva snatches up the scrap of paper. *"Merci,"* she says and slides it into her pocket.

"Don't you think you should open it?" asks Mme Larcher. "It's from Jacques."

Eva stares at her. How can she read a note from Jacques—*a love note*—with his mother sitting right there? Doesn't she understand how impossible that would be?

But apparently Mme Larcher does understand because almost immediately she offers to make them some tea. "It's such a frightful day, I think we need something hot," she says and heads for the kitchen.

When she's gone, Eva pulls the piece of paper out of her pocket, aware that her heart is pounding absurdly. She wishes she could be more dispassionate about Jacques, but it's impossible. She loves him so much that everything having to do with him is somehow amplified. He laces up his boots and she cannot help but admire the brisk way he does it. He kisses the inside of her elbow and the sensation lasts all day. He tells her about the things he's seen on his trips around the city—a car with a wood-burning engine, a pig being fattened in someone's basement, a girl he knows walking arm in arm with a German—and she commits his stories to memory, just so she can have the pleasure of repeating them to herself later on.

She looks down at the note in her lap and tries to calm

herself, but her hands are shaking so much she can barely undo the folds.

* * *

Meanwhile, thirteen-year-old Paul Guérin (it's only a pseudonym, his real name is Benno Breslerman) has been at his workbench sewing pelts for the last couple of hours when M. Liwerant tells him to run over to UGIF. "They should be open by now," he says, "so see if you can't get yourself a bicycle registration card."

Paul wastes no time getting his coat and cap. The idea of a bicycle is irresistible: he sees himself floating down alleys, rounding corners as gracefully as a greyhound, slipping in and out of traffic . . .

"Mind you, though," says M. Liwerant as Paul opens the door, "it's for work only. Deliveries and pick-ups, that's all."

"Of course," replies Paul as he steps into the street, where the wind throws sleet in his face. His coat, which his mother bought him back in Leipzig, is too small now, leaving his wrists sadly exposed. Nonetheless, it's good to get away. M. Liwerant is so unrelentingly gloomy that Paul feels half-dead in his presence. Still, if the old furrier hadn't taken him on as an apprentice, who knows where he'd be? Most likely in Vénissieux or one of Vichy's other internment camps.

He knows they're not run by the Germans, but from what he's heard they might as well be.

* * *

At approximately the same time, Gilberte Jacob, a UGIF social worker who turned thirty only a week ago, is at her desk updating a list of possible lodgings. Some she finds in newspaper ads, but those go to the bottom of her list. Next come apartment buildings where they've placed people in the past; perhaps a room can be found in one of those apartments for a refugee family with nowhere else to go. Then, finally, there are the addresses vacated by former clients who have gone to the Italian zone or managed to cross into Switzerland. It's tedious work, so tedious that when she glances at the clock she can hardly believe that it's only twenty minutes after nine. She leans back in her chair and stretches, her slender arms spread out in a wide "V." She could do with some coffee, she decides, but just as she's about to get some, the door bangs open and five or six men barge into the office. They are wearing long leather coats and broad-brimmed trilbies.

"*Haut les mains,*" yells one of them, lurching toward her with his gun drawn.

Momentarily paralyzed, Gilberte stares at the barrel of the gun, trying to understand. *The Gestapo? But why? UGIF is an authorized agency.*

"I said, hands up," he repeats, grabbing her under one arm and yanking her out of her seat.

Gilberte puts her hands up, and he shoves her against a bank of filing cabinets where one of the drawer handles hits her in the small of her back. The pain is sudden and sharp, and she cries out, her voice just one among many as staff and clients alike are pushed up against the walls.

9:30 in the morning

Eva Gottlieb is still gazing at Jacques's note when Mme Larcher returns with the tea. The message (just a few short words: *Meet me tonight, seven o'clock, you know where*) has revived her. She's not thinking about her cold wet feet or M.

Weissman's sad little orphans now. That's what the prospect of seeing Jacques does for her: all the day-to-day tensions fall away, leaving her on some other plane where she can forget and be young again—as young as any other girl her age.

"*Bonnes nouvelles*, I hope," says Mme Larcher as she hands her pupil a cup of tea.

Eva nods, looking at the delicate blue-and-white cup. It's from Madame's prized set of Meissen—or, rather, what's left of it, since, according to Jacques, she's had to let most of it go (four place settings for a sack of potatoes, a soup tureen for a rabbit which wasn't even skinned). It saddens Eva to think about everything Mme Larcher has lost, but she can't help being gratified by the compliment she is paying her. A year ago, Mme Larcher would never have brought out her blue onion china for Eva. In fact, she probably wouldn't have served tea at all.

It makes Eva think that if she and Jacques ever decided to get married, Mme Larcher might not oppose it. A vast social gulf stretches between Jacques's family and her own, but war is a great leveler. If nothing else, it's brought them together: two young *résistants* who wouldn't have met if it hadn't been for a madman in Berlin ranting about racial purity.

* * *

By now, Obersturmführer Barbie has set himself up at a big desk toward the back of the UGIF's main room where he's busy checking everyone's papers, starting with the staff. He pays particular attention to the women, curious to see how they'll react when Stengritt frisks them.

Stengritt belongs to Section VI, however, so he doesn't go at it with quite the same fervor as the rest of Klaus's men. It doesn't make much difference, though, since the women all seem to age as soon as their pocketbooks are taken away. Their faces sag, their posture droops, their eyes start to wander aimlessly. Klaus can't explain this, but it's something that happens ninety-nine percent of the time. And if you take away a woman's wedding ring (they're not bothering with that now), the effect is even more pronounced.

When all of the female staff has been "processed," Klaus asks which of them is the switchboard operator. Silence follows, but a few furtive glances guide him to a gaunt, frizzy-haired woman who stands toward the back of the group. Klaus, after ascertaining that she is indeed the operator, has her step forward and tells her to behave just as she would on any other day.

"When people call, tell them to come in as usual," he instructs her, and she nods, looking as if he'd told her to put her head in a vise.

* * *

On the narrow street in front of Number 12, André Deutsch, who's just arriving, encounters a scrawny boy whose face is red with cold. "Is this UGIF?" the boy asks, looking around as they both step into the vestibule.

"It is," says André, who's almost knocked over by the boy's pungent odor. André has no idea how a city kid could have picked up this barnyard smell, but he's so relieved to have made it to his destination that he gives it only a moment's thought.

"Follow me," he tells the boy and starts up the stairs, repeating to himself, over and over: *My last trip, it's finished, now I can breathe again.* But then, when they get to the second-floor landing, the door which André is about to reach for swings open, seemingly by itself, to reveal a leather-coated figure holding a pistol. "German police," the man says, stepping forward and dropping a hand onto André's shoulder, while another man, also in leather, grabs hold of the boy. For a split second, André considers wresting himself away—he pictures himself plunging down the stairs and disappearing into a *traboule*—but just as quickly he realizes how pointless that would be.

"Hand it over," says the German, pointing to André's briefcase. André complies—what choice does he have?—then watches as the Boche struggles with the clasps. "It's locked," he finally announces, looking up at André as if he's never encountered an impediment of this sort.

André nods. "Yes," he murmurs, his mind so foggy it's as if he's dreaming.

"Well, are you going to give me the key or not?" the German demands, waving his pistol in André's face.

With an effort, André tries to focus. "It's in . . . in my . . . in here," he says, fumbling under his coat and suit jacket for the key that's buried in his waistcoat pocket.

"Well, hurry up," says the German, ramming his pistol into the side of André's neck. André, feeling the cold metal of the barrel against his skin, finally manages to produce the key with shaking fingers. He holds it out on the palm of his hand, and the German snatches it up.

Then, only moments later, he's whistling for his boss. "*Chef*, you gotta see this," he yells, smiling broadly enough for André to see his long yellowish teeth. "There must be at least twenty or thirty thousand francs in here!"

10 o'clock in the morning

A vicious wind slams into Eva Gottlieb as she struggles toward rue Sainte-Catherine, but she's too preoccupied with thoughts about Jacques to feel the cold. It's been almost two weeks since they've seen each other, and she worries, just as she always does, that something might have happened during that time to diminish his interest in her. She tries to talk sense to herself (*has anything diminished her ardor? No, of course not*), but these days she doesn't trust the solidity of anyone or anything. She doesn't trust UGIF to protect the names of their foster mothers. She doesn't trust the Szulklaper brothers, or at least not Victor. And she certainly doesn't trust the exemption cards handed out by the Boches. They're supposed to protect UGIF staff and their families from "all internment measures," but Eva is doubtful. Her mother has one, and though it probably gives her a bit of extra confidence, Eva wishes she had a false ID instead.

It was Esther Grinberg, one of the administrators, who got Eva hers, but neither Mlle Grinberg nor anyone else at UGIF would authorize a false ID for Eva's mother. There were more pressing needs, Eva was told: her mother was always at her desk, never leaving the office, not even for lunch, while there were others (Eva herself, for instance) who were so exposed they wouldn't last a week without a French ID.

Eva has thought about getting her mother a card on the black market, but when she asked Victor if he could use his connections to help her get one, he told her a fake ID, if it was good, would cost as much as a refrigerator. After that Eva gave up, but now, just as she's crossing the pont Morand, it occurs to her that Victor might have been lying. Perhaps, if you knew the right person, the price could be negotiated.

She'll ask Jacques about it tonight, she decides, glancing down at the Saône River below her. Generally, the river's as placid as bath water, but today, because it's being whipped by the wind, it looks darkly threatening. This could be a warning if Eva chose to take it that way, but she barely notices. Instead, she's thinking about Jacques and the night ahead: how she'll knock and then he'll come to the door with his arms outstretched, instantly shutting out all the things she's afraid of: the German checkpoints, the babies that won't stop crying, the Alsatians on leashes that rip open the night with their barking.

* * *

Paul Guérin, the furrier's apprentice, looks around the room where the Germans have shoved him. He is still smarting from his encounter with the pockmarked guy at the door who started knocking him around the minute he walked in. "Dirty Jew," the man had snarled, "you smell like a cesspool." The blows hadn't bothered Paul much—M. Liwerant is quick with his fists as well—but being told that he stinks was like having a knife sunk into his gut. Because how can he help it working with all those unwashed sheepskins? Of course, the odor was going to soak into his pores. There wasn't much he could do about it.

The room is crowded, so crowded Paul doesn't know if he'll be able to find a place for himself. But then, glancing around the room, he sees a teenaged girl who reminds him of his sister. Cheered by the sight of someone who seems so familiar, he starts to sit down on the floor beside her only to have her hold her nose and turn away as if he were contagion itself.

Feeling more than ever like a pariah, Paul searches the room again, but there's no one who will even look at him. The exclusion is so complete he's afraid he'll start crying, but then he spots the small bearded man he came in with and works his way over to him. "*Je peux?*" he asks politely, gesturing toward a spot on the floor beside him. There's a moment's hesitation and Paul braces himself for another rejection, but then a look of resignation passes over the man's face and he scoots over to make room beside him.

* * *

Meanwhile, in the nearby suburb of Caluire, nineteen-year-old
Chana Grinzpan slips out of her room and knocks on Edzia
Rozenfarb's door which is just one over from hers. Edzia was
the first friend Chana made after fleeing Poland two years ago.
They'd met in Paris where each of them lived in a flat backing
up to the Passage Alexandrine: Mme Rozenfarb and her teen-
aged daughter on one side, Chana and her husband and their
new baby on the other. To carry on conversations, all the two
women had to do was open their back windows and yell across
the alleyway. But then Chana's husband was rounded up
during the Vel d'Hiv *rafle*, and the two friends, frightened of
being arrested themselves, had pooled their funds and come
here, to Lyon, which (at that time anyway) had seemed like a
refuge.

Chana waits, then knocks again. "Edzia," she says, pressing
her lips to the wood of the door.

A moment later the door opens a crack and Chana pushes
her way in. "Edzia, you have to help me," she says, her voice
breaking a little.

Edzia turns off the hotplate on which she's boiling some
groats. "Of course, but please, keep your voice down. Jacqueline's still asleep."

Chana looks over at the divan where Edzia's fourteen-year-
old daughter is sleeping and nods. Chana doesn't much care
whether she wakes Jacqueline or not (what kind of princess is
she, still asleep at this time of the morning?), but all the same
she lowers her voice. "It's the baby," she whispers. "He's sick
again."

"Oh, no," says Edzia, a worried look crossing her broad
comfortable face. "It's not serious, is it?"

Chana considers. "No, I don't think so. An earache maybe.

But he should see a doctor, and I don't know . . ." Her voice trails off and she shrugs her shoulders.

For a moment, Edzia looks at Chana (really, she could pass for a twelve-year-old, a girl still waiting for her breasts to sprout) and considers her dilemma. "But wait, isn't this assistance day?"

"At UGIF, you mean?"

"Yes, it's Monday, isn't it? The doctor will be there along with that nice nurse of his—Marcelle, isn't that her name? She'll help you, I'm sure."

Chana considers this. Marcelle *is* nice and so is Dr Lanzenberg, though he has a way of scowling at you the whole time you're talking to him. But she knows that he's a good doctor.

"All right," she says finally, "but won't you come with me?"

Edzia sighs. "Chana, you know I have to work. It's not much but . . ."

"I know," says Chana, and she does. The small salary Edzia earns by checking out customers in a garment shop allows them to buy a few extra vegetables each month along with some pabulum for Rene. "I just wish . . . I mean, it's so far, and you know the Métro . . . sometimes there are checkpoints."

Edzia frowns and wipes her hands on her apron. "Chana, really—" she begins, then stops herself.

"I know," says Chana, sinking onto a chair, "you think I'm useless, a coward when it comes to—"

"No, I do not think you're a coward," says Edzia, raising her voice to a normal pitch. "We're all afraid to go out on the streets. You'd have to be a fool not to be." She pauses for a moment, then continues: "But, Chana, you're the mother. You have to take responsibility. You do understand that, don't you?"

Chana looks down at her lap. She knows Edzia is right. She has to do the best she can for René, but why does she have to risk her life just to get a little medicine?

She is about to say as much, but just then the figure on the couch stirs, and they both look over at Jacqueline, who sits up and blinks at them with bleary eyes. "Chana, is that you?" she asks.

"Who else would it be, you sleepy head?" chides Chana, causing Edzia to smile. Chana may be five years older than Jacqueline, but the two girls are like sisters, teasing one another the way Edzia and her sisters had. And for a moment, Edzia permits herself to think about them. Edzia herself had been able to slip out of the ghetto in Lodz just before it was sealed, but her two sisters and their families . . . well, she just doesn't know.

Edzia looks from her daughter to Chana wishing she could build a wall around them to keep them safe when an idea comes to her. "Chana, why don't you wait until this afternoon to go to UGIF? Then Jacqueline could meet you there after her class and the two of you could come home together." Edzia worries about Jacqueline coming home after dark, and she knows that both girls will be safer if they're together.

Chana quickly agrees. "What a good idea," she says, looking over at Jacqueline who never draws undue attention because she's as French as any *jeune fille* born and raised in Lyon.

She speaks French without an accent. She wears her hair rolled back from her temples. She even takes apart her mother's old dresses and remakes them in the latest styles (short hemlines, broad shoulders, a felt corsage: she knows just what to do, thanks to her couture class). It's really quite amazing.

"So it's set then," says Edzia, looking at the two girls who have settled side by side on the divan to work out the details.

"*Mais oui,*" answers Jacqueline, smiling back at her mother like the angel she is.

10:30 in the morning

A deep sense of gloom descends on Maier Weissman as more and more people are shoved into the back room. People he knows, people who have been coming in month after month, anxious or sometimes belligerent, but almost always embarrassed to find themselves at a welfare agency like UGIF.

Huddled in the corner next to a bin of old clothes are the Taubmanns, refugees from Austria who would much prefer to work than rely on hand-outs. Beno, their thirty-two-year-old son, helps out by giving private lessons in German, but he doesn't earn much. What he needs are some *lycée* professors willing to refer their students, but so far none of them have.

And there, under the window, with his worn overcoat wrapped around him, is Jacques Peskind, a Latvian in his sixties whose French doesn't go much beyond *"Merci beaucoup"* and *"Je ne comprends pas."* In Riga he'd been a machinist; now he peddles newspapers and mourns his family.

And over there, standing beside some of the secretaries, is Erna Freund, who'd been a professional singer in Hungary. It's hardest for people like her. They'd always had money so they never learned to negotiate (no, it was easier just to pay the price). But now, here in Lyon, negotiating is all they ever do: *Can't I stay a few more days in this hotel? Won't this ring (look, that's a real ruby) do for the rent?*

* * *

As soon as Eva Gottlieb opens the door to the office, a pockmarked man with heavy hands starts searching her. Eva, who's more confused than frightened, looks around for her mother—*where is she!*—but the heavy-handed man redirects her attention with a vigorous slap.

Automatically, Eva's hand flies up to her cheek, but she drops it immediately, realizing that a reaction is probably just what he wants. Well, he won't get one from her, she vows, forcing herself to watch dispassionately as he dumps the contents of her rucksack onto a nearby desk. He fishes out her ID and *carte d'alimentation* and hands them back to her, then starts poking through the rest of her things: two pencils and a pad of paper, her wallet containing a few francs and a coin or two, a tube of lipstick, a comb and some hair pins, a copy of the New Testament, a box of matches and a ball of string, a pair of child's mittens—and the sheet music from her lesson, which the *gestapiste* picks up and studies.

But this is too much for Eva. The rest of her things, yes, he can have them, but not the Beethoven. It's not even hers, but Gilberte Jacob's. "Please, I need that," she says and holds out her hand.

"You mean this?" asks the man in clumsy French, dangling the music in front of her.

Eva stares at him, taking in the grin on his face—a grin so ghoulish it reminds her of a skull—and snatches the music out of his hand. Then, not knowing what else to do, she rolls it up and slips it inside the sleeve of her coat. There, gone, out of sight.

The ghoul, having watched her little performance, shrugs his shoulders. "You want it so much, then go ahead, keep it," he says and pushes her towards a desk at the back of the room where a man in a pinstriped suit is waiting.

* * *

Meanwhile, Marcelle Loeb is struggling to keep up with Dr Lanzenberg as he strides across the place des Terreaux with a warrior's stoic expression on his face. Some people consider him fractious, and in a way maybe he is, but he's never angry at his patients, only at the conditions they have to put up with: malnutrition, overcrowding, poverty, and, most of all, fear. Just this morning there was an emergency: a woman, in labor almost four days, with a husband too afraid to send for a doctor. It's that sort of thing that enrages Dr Lanzenberg, because what could be worse—the poor woman's in agony and the baby, of course, is dead. He ended up having to pull it out with forceps. Marcelle knows how distressing that was for him, but it was distressing for her too. She wishes he would talk to her about it. But she knows that he won't because she's only nineteen and not a real nurse, just a nursing assistant.

He, on the other hand, had been the *chef de clinique dermatologique* in Strasbourg.

When they come abreast of the fountain with its galloping steeds, Dr Lanzenberg gestures toward a nearby *pharmacie.* Yelling to make himself heard over the wind, he asks her to buy some gauze pads and eyewash while he goes ahead to rue Sainte-Catherine.

Marcelle is dumbfounded. On a day like today when her feet are so numb they feel cut off from her body, he wants her to go shopping for incidentals? But she doesn't argue with him. She's tried it before and it only confuses him: he simply doesn't understand why his orders would need to be reviewed.

* * *

Eva Gottlieb had hoped that the man in the pinstriped suit would let her go as soon as she handed over her documents and he saw that she had a French ID. But he only glances at her papers before confiscating them and ordering her into the back room where twenty or thirty people are bunched together on one side of the room. Eva is told to sit on the opposite side, however, which, except for a couple of people she doesn't know, is unoccupied. Sitting down on the nearest chair, she frantically scans the room for her mother, but it takes a moment or two before she spots her standing in the corner next to Mme Freund, her Hungarian friend.

Eva, who is so relieved that she forgets where she is, smiles broadly and even waves. That's how glad she is to see her mother. Actually, if she could, she'd like to sit down with her right now and tell her all about Mme Larcher and how she brought out her best china for Eva and doesn't her mother think that's encouraging... But Eva's mother only frowns and gives a small shake of her head. At first Eva is puzzled but then she notices the guard standing just inside the door and decides that her mother is right. It's probably better if he doesn't catch on to their real relationship, because what would happen if he compared their IDs—one in the name of Aurélie Gottlieb, the other (Eva's) in the name of Edmée Gardier? It wouldn't make sense for two people with such different last names (and different addresses) to be related in any way. In fact, it would be a sure tip-off that one of their cards was fake.

Eva isn't particularly worried, though. She imagines that some people will be hauled away for transport to one of the internment camps, or perhaps even to Drancy, the transit camp just outside Paris, but she's confident that she and her mother will both be released. Why wouldn't they be? She has a French ID, and her mother's exemption card, as far as Eva knows, is still good.

*　*　*

Several miles away in the working-class suburb of Villeurbanne, Victor Szulkapler and his older brother, Rachmil, are boarding the Métro on their way to see Weissman at UGIF.

Rachmil is employed there: he even has an exemption card which says so. But his real work (not noted on the card) is helping Eva Gottlieb and her team smuggle Jews into Switzerland. Victor is an occasional *passeur* as well, but his smuggling interests go beyond Jewish children. Cognac, cigarettes, silk stockings and other luxury items: that's what keeps the family in potatoes.

A few of the Métro passengers are students, but the majority of riders are housewives with string bags who are on the hunt for a couple of eggs or a sliver of beef. All of them, though, whether young or old, have a gray, desiccated look.

Still, there's one girl—a teenager with curly red hair—who gets Victor's attention. She's an audacious little thing, sitting there as cool as you please, applying lipstick as if no one was watching. And it's not a virginal color either, like peach or pink, but a bright cannibalistic red. He stares until Rach pokes him in the ribs. "You could take a picture, it would last longer," he says under his breath in Polish.

Victor snaps out of his trance and looks at his brother. "*Française,*" he says automatically. "*Parlez française.*"

Noon

André Deutsch looks over at Maier Weissman, who's sitting on the floor wiping the sweat from his face and neck with a handkerchief. André is worried about him. The man has a heart condition and, clearly, he's not doing too well. But at least he's not sitting next to a boy who stinks to high heaven the way André is. But of course, it's not the kid's fault. He didn't know that the Germans were going to be here anymore than André did.

André doesn't think this is a standard *rafle*, however. His guess is they're looking for someone specific. Someone from the Resistance like Eva Gottlieb, who's essential to the Swiss *filière*, or Michel Kroskof who routinely stops by to recruit Jews for the *Armée secrète*. And what about the Szulkapler brothers? André isn't sure what they're mixed up in, but he knows it has something to do with the black market, which is just as illegal as passing out subversive pamphlets or pouring sugar into the gas tanks of German vehicles.

Not that André wants Eva or Michel or even the Szulkaplers to be arrested, he doesn't. But if they were, then the rest of them might be able to go home, shaken but none the worse for wear.

And Savoie would still be there, waiting for him.

* * *

Because of where she is sitting (directly across from the room's open doorway), Eva Gottlieb is able to see her friend Marcelle Loeb when she arrives. Eva had hoped when Dr Lanzenberg came in by himself, that Marcelle was taking the day off or busy elsewhere, but here she is, cheeks pink from the cold, her arms full of parcels. Eva can see that she's startled by the sight of the Gestapo, but if she's afraid she manages to hide it well, even when the ghoul comes forward to frisk her. But then nurses are almost always calm, reflects Eva, watching as Marcelle is pushed in the direction of the pinstriped *chef*.

"*Votre carte d'identité, s'il vous plait,*" the man says, sounding more like a bureaucrat than a Gestapo agent.

But Marcelle isn't paying attention. Instead, her eyes are fixed on Dr Lanzenberg's bag which is lying on its side amidst a pile of discarded pocketbooks and rucksacks. Seeing it there, looking so forlorn and useless, she feels a sudden weakness wash over her. How will Dr Lanzenberg ever function without it? It's as much a part of him as his arm or his leg.

"*Votre carte,*" repeats the *chef*, this time more brusquely, and Marcelle, with an effort, turns her attention to him.

"*Oui, m'sieur,*" she says and hands over her things: first her papers, then her pocketbook, and then, last of all, the parcels containing the gauze pads and eyewash.

* * *

When the Szulkaplers come in a little later, dressed in their berets and jackboots, André Deutsch feels almost giddy. Just look at them, he thinks. Any fool can see they're up to no good.

He holds his breath, watching as the man at the door, the one with the pockmarked face and wolfish teeth, takes his time examining their IDs. He even calls over the pinstriped man for a consultation, but in the end it comes to nothing. The brothers are searched, relieved of their knives and brass knuckles, then waved into the back room along with everybody else.

André is devastated. They're black-market operators, aren't they, so why weren't they handcuffed and dragged off immediately?

It just doesn't make sense.

* * *

A little after that, Eva Gottlieb hears one of the *gestapistes* yelling out in German: "Look, here's another Jewish kitten, and this one's a redhead." It's her ghoul of course, busy harassing a pretty *jeune fille*, who, in spite of the dark red lipstick she wears, can't be more than sixteen. Eva isn't sure if she understands German, but judging by the horrified look on her face, Eva guesses she does. Still, when asked for her name, she's cagey enough to answer in French. *"Je m'appelle Lea Katz,"* she tells him, backing out of the door as she says it and babbling that she must have the wrong office.

"You see, my mother is very sick, and I'm looking for a doctor," she adds, amazed at how easily these words fall from her lips since the real reason she's here is much more venal. "I have no idea what's wrong with her," she continues, "but she has these horrible pains. I think it might be appendicitis."

But the ghoul isn't interested in her sob story. He grabs her by the arm and yanks her back into the office where his big hands go under her coat, aggressively patting her breasts, her hips, whatever else he can reach. She holds her breath while this is happening (as if that would help), but she knows she has no one to blame but herself. What was she thinking anyway, running after those two flashy gangsters? Even now she isn't quite certain what her plan had been, but she'd seen one of them (the one with the mustache) looking at her and she'd known that it wouldn't be hard to chat them up, to flirt with them just enough to enjoy a bit of their largesse. And, besides, she hadn't wanted that much: just a pair of silk stockings or a nice meal at Mere Brazier's. Either would have been plenty.

2 o'clock in the afternoon

Panting a little after her run from the Métro station, Chana Grinzspan pauses for a moment in front of the UGIF office to collect herself. She pushes at her hair, which is wet from the snow, then unpeels some of the sweaters and scarves that she's wrapped around René.

Looking into his red little face—*You're feverish, aren't you?*—she feels something come loose inside her. If her baby should die after all she's been through with him—the Vel' d' Hive roundup, the hazardous trip across the *ligne de demarcation*—then why bother going on? She presses her baby's hot cheek against her own and he whimpers weakly. Then, turning toward the door, she reaches for the handle, but no sooner has she touched it than the door opens by itself. And then a man—she knows he's Gestapo—takes her by the shoulder and tells her she's under arrest.

* * *

Maier Weissman is feeling faint and there's a constant ache in the small of his back, though perhaps that's good since it keeps him from thinking too much about the reality of his situation. But there's no pain in the world that can keep him from thinking about his family.

About Miriam, for instance, whose birthday it is. She is sixty-two, not so old really, but he knows that she feels old (as does he, older and older every day). And then there's Sylvie, their daughter: pretty, yes, but smart, too, good at languages especially, picking them up without any effort at all. It's a shame she couldn't have gone to university, but in times like these, well . . . yet marriage wasn't the answer either. Because even if her husband is alive somewhere, he's not with his family where he's needed. It makes Maier sad to think about little Ezekiel growing up without a father, or possibly any male presence at all, if he, the grandfather, is also deported. But Maier pushes that thought away, returning instead to his wife's birthday and the cake that Sylvie is probably icing right now.

Maier had worked hard to make that cake possible, begging a bit of sugar from four different friends in return for an invitation to the "party," trading his gold cufflinks for the eggs and the cream, and then, because he had no other choice, turning to the Szulkaplers for the chocolate, a commodity so rare it might as well be manna. But the important thing is that Miriam will have her cake, and even if he's not there to see it, nothing the Germans or Vichy can do now will interfere with that.

* * *

When Michel Krostof, the *Armée secrète* recruiter, arrives at UGIF, he is greeted by a pockmarked Boche who yells out, "*Kommen Sie herein!*" Michel is shocked but not especially frightened since he carries an ID in the name of Sberro. When you've been detained in a place like Les Milles, you learn that being afraid is a waste of energy. Better to be reckless instead. If he hadn't been, he'd still be there, instead of with the *Armée secrète* in Grenoble.

Quickly, Michel pulls out his portfolio and begins his spiel: *He's a poor artist, here to sell a few drawings, might you be interested, monsieur?* He even takes out two or three of his sketches —he's not a bad draftsman—and shows them to the man.

Eva, who is slightly acquainted with Michel through Jacques, is impressed with this performance. But then she remembers what Jacques once said: he's a chameleon par excellence. It wasn't exactly a compliment, but she understands what he meant when she sees the German leaning over one of Michel's drawings.

Michel, who is just as surprised as Eva by this show of interest, actually starts to calculate a price in his head (who knows, maybe the man likes cathedrals), but then, before they can get any further, the Boche shoves him toward a big desk at the back of the room. "We must introduce you to the top man," he says, pointing to the guy in a pinstriped suit.

Looking at him, Michel thinks there's something familiar about him, though he can't put his finger on it. But then, a moment later, it comes to him: *this is Klaus Barbie, the so-called*

Butcher of Lyon! He knows because once, when he and Jacques were walking along rue Merciere, Jacques pointed him out and said, "Notice how everybody jumps out of his way?

"That's how you know it's Barbie."

Seen at close range, however, *le boucher* is less impressive than expected. The girlish complexion is bad enough (honestly, he's as pink as a pig), but the silly blond quiff is even worse. Still, Michel has heard enough about the man's methods—the electrodes, the dogs, the *baignoires*—to feel a bit nervous. But Barbie isn't interested in Michel. He takes only a cursory glance at his papers, then waves him into the next room, where he's directed to sit on the left-hand side with a handful of others. One of them, he's surprised to see, is Jacques's girl-friend. Having met her only a couple of times, he can't remember her name, but he gives her a small nod just for the sake of solidarity.

* * *

Eva Gottlieb returns Michel Krostof's nod but can't help cringing inwardly. She doesn't like being linked with him—or with Victor Szulklaper either. They're too active, too visible, too flamboyant. But then it occurs to her that she *is* linked with them because here they all are, lined up together on the same side of the room with only a handful of others. If the one thing they all have in common is a French ID (which is what she assumes), then separating them makes sense. But what if that's not the reason? What if the Germans have somehow found out about their illicit activities and are holding them as suspects?

The thought throws her into a panic. She doesn't know first-hand what goes on at the hôtel Terminus, but she's heard plenty of stories from Jacques's friends. How they inject acid into people's bladders. How they use the hotel's fancy bathtubs to hold people's heads under water until they're on the verge of drowning. How they have dogs that are trained to do unspeakable things to the female prisoners.

No!

She can't think about this, it's too appalling. She takes a few deep breaths, then forces herself to think about something else entirely: the ingredients for bouillabaisse, the kings of France going back to Philip II, the names of all her cousins in alphabetical order. But nothing helps. Her mind keeps sliding back to the hôtel Terminus.

Suddenly, though, she remembers the Beethoven scores. Why not study those? They're certainly intricate enough. She picks up her coat from the floor and pulls the sheet music out of the sleeve. Looking down at "Für Elise," Eva can hardly believe that she'd been playing (or trying to play) it for Mme Larcher only that morning. Madame had winced at every wrong note, but she hadn't interrupted once—quite unusual for her since she generally had plenty to say. But the only things Mme Larcher said today were: "More emotion if you will" and "Eva, please, try to let yourself go."

4 o'clock in the afternoon

Deciding it's time to take matters into his own hands, Victor Szulkapler, the smuggler and occasional *passeur*, walks over to one of the Germans to tell him that he needs to go the lavatory. "A bad case of diarrhea," he warns, and that's enough, the Boche lets him go. Once inside the lavatory, Victor takes a deep breath and reminds himself that now is not the time to be sentimental. Sure, he'd like to save his brother, but how is he supposed to do that? Rachmil can't speak French worth a shit and he carries around an ID bearing his real name. Victor's ID, on the other hand, is in the name of Francois-Victor Sordier—a good French name that's common, but not too common. Using a bit of soap, Victor struggles to remove his pinky ring, but he can't get it to budge. It's almost as if the ring has become a part of his flesh. But finally, by holding his finger under cold running water and applying still more soap, he's able to ease it past his knuckle and slide it off his finger. It's too bad, he thinks, as he hides the ring behind a loose baseboard, because the diamond is real, but Rach has a ring just like it so he doesn't dare keep it.

* * *

Chana Grinzspan's baby is starting to fuss. She lets him suck on her finger, but she knows he's hungry. Not only that, but she can feel her milk letting down, wetting the blouse she wears under her sweater. She looks over at Marcelle Loeb who is standing nearby—Marcelle, the doctor's assistant who always knows the right thing to do—but she can tell by the look on her face that Marcelle is frightened too. Hugging René close to her, Chana feels her stomach shrinking. If even Marcelle is scared, then they must all be doomed.

* * *

When he returns from the lavatory, Victor Szulkapler catches Rach's eye just long enough to make it clear that, from here on out, they're no longer brothers. In fact, they don't even know each other. Then, with as casual an air as possible, he approaches the German called Stengritt, choosing him because he seems to be at least moderately intelligent and not quite as much of a *Schweinhund* as the others.

"*S'il vous plaît, monsieur,*" he says in a nonchalant tone

with just a hint of pugnacity in it, "but how much longer am I going to have to sit here?" He looks at his watch in mock frustration and continues: "I mean, it's been three hours already, and I don't know about you, but I have work to do." He pauses. "Besides, I'm French, not Jewish. The only reason I came here today was to meet a friend—a friend who never even showed up."

Eva Gottlieb, who is watching this, looks over at Michel Kroskof, her fellow *résistant*, knowing that he's thinking the same thing she is: if the Gestapo lets Victor go, there's reason to hope, but if they don't . . . well, who knows.

Together, they watch intently as the yellow-haired German retrieves the stack of confiscated documents from the *chef* and starts going through them. Victor, standing on the sidelines, seems impressively blasé while this is going on, but what they don't know is that it's only a pose. In reality, every cell in Victor's body is trembling. He's reasonably certain his *carte d'identité* is good—it should be since he paid dearly for it, but you never know— sometimes there's a small inconsistency or a stamp that's missing—it's ridiculous how much Germans love their stamps, everything always has to be so official with them— it makes it hard for the counterfeiters . . . But at last, Stengritt locates Victor's papers and declares them to be in order.

"What a country," he says as he hands them to Victor. "You can't even tell a Jew from a Gentile." Victor has no idea what this means—*Do they know his card is a fake? Is that the message?*—but he keeps his face as mask-like as possible, waiting until he's on the sidewalk in front of Number 12 before permitting himself to breathe again.

* * *

In spite of the slushy streets, only half-cleared of snow, Jacqueline Rozenfarb is buoyant as she walks along rue Sainte-Catherine to meet Chana Grinzspan. When Jacqueline started her couture course, she hadn't expected to be the star of the class (she'd never even thought she had much aptitude for sewing), yet somehow her fingers seem made for this work and no one gets as much attention from Mme Doucet as she does. Today, for instance, they had to set sleeves into armholes. For most of the girls, it was tedious work, pinning, basting, clipping, then ripping the whole thing out and doing it all over again because Madame was so hard to please.

But Jacqueline had no trouble. She was able to ease her wool crepe sleeve into place after only one try and without so much as a single pucker. Mme Doucet actually stopped the class so she could show them Jacqueline's work. The other girls stared at her, some of them resentfully, but Jacqueline hung her head and did her best to look embarrassed. The praise was as welcome as sunshine, but she couldn't afford to be arrogant, not with a name like Rozenfarb.

Almost all of the light has gone out of the sky by the time Jacqueline arrives at Number 12, which always strikes her as dismal, even a little ominous. Inside the foyer, she pauses a moment to blow on her poor frozen fingers, then starts up the stairs which are so dimly lit she practically has to feel her way up them. The building seems quiet, much quieter than on past visits, but it's a soothing kind of quiet, permitting her thoughts to slide back to Mme Doucet.

In the beginning, Jacqueline had been terrified of her. She was so tall and austere and pulled her hair back into such a tight little chignon it was hard to believe that anything would ever please her. And of course she's still this way, except now she's the *artiste* Jaqueline wants to become. Someday the war will end—it has to—and then she and her mother, and maybe

Chana too, will go back to Paris, and Jacqueline will be able to get a job in one of the *ateliers*, Chanel's perhaps, because she's bound to reopen, or if she doesn't then one of the others, Scaparelli's, for instance, or Balenciaga's or . . .

But she is wrenched out of her reverie as soon as she opens the door to the office and sees a man with a gun in his hand. She is so startled that for several moments she's unable to move or speak or even take in what is happening. *A gun? Really? And it's pointed at me?*

"*Juif?*" asks the man, smirking as he looks her over. His teeth, she notices, are long and yellow, like a dog's.

"*Française,*" she replies, and it's not a lie, she really has become French. Poland is so long ago, she can't even remember it.

He looks her over once more, then asks again, "*Mais, Juif?*"

There's a hint of confusion in his question, however, and once again she answers, this time even more confidently, "*Non, Française.*"

Unfortunately, though, her ID says otherwise, and she is pointed in the direction of the back room where she is told to wait. Confused, she looks from one side of the room to the other, unable to understand. Who are all these people—sixty or seventy of them at least—and what are they doing here, packed together like riders on the Métro? Then she hears a baby crying and, turning toward the sound, sees Chana standing next to the window with little René. She tries to guess from Chana's face what's going on, but all she sees there is terror.

A cold sick feeling goes through her then as a voice from within tells her this is the end. She will never finish her class now, never see her mother again, never even live to be fifteen. But then, just as the room around her is starting to spin, a petite young woman comes forward and takes her by the hand.

"Why don't you come sit by me?" she says, but Jacqueline

is too frightened to respond. "It's all right," adds the woman, squeezing her hand. "My name is Gilberte Jacob. I'm a social worker."

5 o'clock in the evening

Redheaded Lea Katz is sitting on the floor next to M. Weissman, and she knows he is doing his best to calm her: a pat on the knee, a less-than-convincing smile whenever he thinks to look her way. But it doesn't help. It's nearing the end of the day and everyone is restless. Some are praying, others weeping. People come up to M. Weissman and murmur into his ear— *What will they do? Send us to a camp? Let us go? Take the men, leave the women?*—but M. Weissman only shrugs his shoulders. He doesn't know any more than they do.

Chana Grinzspan is beside herself. She's tried everything she can think of to calm René—rocking him in her arms, hoisting him over her shoulder, massaging his belly—but nothing helps, he just won't stop crying.

And the Boches are losing patience, especially that yellow-haired man. Catching one of his sour looks, Chana starts jostling René desperately (*Please, little baby, be good*), then presses his furious face to her bosom in an effort to muffle his screams. But it's too late, the man is already elbowing his way toward her.

"What's wrong with the kid?" he asks in French.

But Chana is too petrified to answer. She backs away, afraid that he'll take René, or even pull out a pistol and shoot him.

But he only repeats the question, and this time Chana manages an answer. "He's hungry, that's all," she says, her voice quivering.

The German shakes his head and says, *"Puis allez lui donnez du chaud."*

Chana stands there, dazed. Is he telling her to go and get her baby some hot food? Is that really what he means? But then he gestures toward the door and gives her a little shove, so it's clear, even to her, that she's being released. She quickly wraps up René while he finds her ID, then heads for the door, plunging through the crowd like a woman running from a fire. At the last moment, though, she turns and looks back at Jacqueline Rozenfarb, wondering how she'll ever explain this to Jacqueline's mother (*I escaped, but, sorry, I had to leave your daughter behind?*). It's only a fleeting thought, though, because Chana knows that there's no time to lose. She's got to get out of here—right now, this very instant—before the Boches change their minds and drag her back.

* * *

At five-thirty, as Obersturmführer Barbie is making one last tour of the back room, he notices a mousy young girl whose head is bent over something in her lap. He can't tell what it is, but she's so completely engrossed in it that she seems to float inside a peaceful space belonging to her alone. Curious, he moves closer, then sees that it's sheet music.

"This is yours?" he asks, picking up the music from her lap without bothering to ask her permission.

"No, not exactly, I borrowed it from a friend," she stammers as he looks down at what is the score for "Für Elise," a piece his mother taught him. Not that he was ever much of a piano player—he wasn't, he simply didn't have her touch—but it was one of her favorites and so he'd kept at it. It's the only serious piece of music he ever committed to memory. Strange that he'd run into it here, he thinks, turning the pages and following the melody until, at some point, he starts to hum it.

Eva, who is watching from the corner of her eye, is amazed. If she's going to plead her case then the time is now.

"That's what I've been working on," she ventures, making an awkward stab at conversation. He doesn't reply, though, so she tries again: "At my lesson, I mean. It was just this morning, before I came here."

He glances at her briefly. "*Compris,*" he says and returns to the music.

Frustrated, Eva decides on a more direct tack. "But, *monsieur,* don't you recall that I am French? If only you'd take another look at my ID, you'd see . . ."

Her voice trails off and Klaus looks down at her, noticing that her skin is so pale he can see the web of blue veins at her temple. "But if you're French, what are you doing here?" he says. "This is a Jewish agency."

"I know, but I had to return the music I'd borrowed."

Klaus regards this as an unlikely excuse. "Who'd you borrow it from?" he asks. "Is that person here?"

The girl looks uncomfortable and for several long moments says nothing. Eventually, though, she points to a young sparrow-like woman on the opposite side of the room whose name, she says, is Gilberte.

Klaus crosses the room and stands in front of her. "So tell me, Gilberte, is this music yours?"

"*Oui, monsieur,*" says Gilberte, looking directly at him. "We both study with Mme Larcher." Then, after a pause, she adds, "Perhaps you've heard of her. She is a remarkable teacher."

The conversational way she says this—as if they were at a

party, as if she were advising him to take lessons too—startles Klaus and he stands back to take a better look at this puny, insolent woman. He's on the verge of slapping her (the Jews, they always think they're so clever), but she quickly bows her head and he makes do with a grunt instead. He thrusts the music at her. "Here, take it," he says and walks back to the Beethoven girl.

"So you're French, are you?" he asks, surveying her carefully. It is possible that she's here just by chance, just as she claims, but he still thinks she's as Jewish as anyone else in this room.

"If only you'd check my ID, then you'd see—"

"*Ja, ja,*" he replies impatiently. "But what do *you* say?"

"My name is Edmée Gardier, *monsieur,* and I was born in Saint-Pierreville, just two hours south of here. That makes me French." It is a stout response, but beneath the starchiness of her voice Klaus can detect a slight tremor.

"So how long have you been taking lessons?"

"Lessons?"

"The piano. If you've worked your way up to Beethoven, you must be serious."

Eva is about to say that she's mediocre, not much of a student at all, but then she catches on and says, "*Oui, monsieur.* Music is my passion."

"Ach," is all he says, but she can tell he's debating her case. Elation bubbles up inside her and she thinks fleetingly about Jacques, who is probably waiting for her right now at his cousin's flat. It's late, almost six o'clock, and the flat is on avenue Berthelot, way over on the other side of the Rhône, but if she leaves right away she won't be terribly late, and Jacques will wait for her, she's sure of that . . .

"Yes, all right," the Gestapo *chef* says finally, scowling at her. "Just pick up your papers from Stengritt"—he points to the tall blond-headed man—"and then you can go."

But suddenly Eva isn't sure. She wants to leave, of course she does, but what about her mother? She can't just walk out and leave her behind, can she? Eva is still reasonably certain that even if they arrest everybody else they'll still let the staff go, but what if she's wrong? Then she might never see her mother again. Eva steals a quick peek at her mother, but her mother's face is insistent: *Don't throw away this chance, Eva. Go now before you lose your nerve.* Still Eva hesitates. Her father is gone now, her brother too, and she doesn't want to be alone, she can't be! It would be unbearable. She looks down at the floor and back again at her mother, who this time goes so far as to shake her head. It's a very minimal shake, but the *chef* still sees it.

"What's the problem?" he asks. "Do you know this woman? Is she related to you?"

"*Non, bien sur que non,*" Eva insists, but something inside her stops. Staying would be so easy. It would require nothing of her, just a quiet submission, that's all. And then everything would be over: no more hiding babies in rucksacks, no more waiting in ditches for patrols to pass, no more barking dogs straining on leashes. She glances at the door and thinks how far away it is, impossibly far. And her feet are so heavy, too heavy even to lift. No, better to stay and be here with her mother. Family is the only thing that matters now.

But then an image of Jacques floats into her mind. She sees him quite clearly—the thick dark hair (such lovely hair), the impudent grin, the eyetooth that projects just a little—and she suddenly realizes that everyone here, even her mother, belongs to the past. Only Jacques can offer her a future: a home, a family, a place for herself on this earth when the fighting is over.

"Well, are you going or not?" asks the *chef.* His tone is menacing.

Eva looks at him blankly. *"Oui, monsieur,"* she says, so detached from this moment that she seems to be watching the scene from above. She sees the Nazi in his pinstriped suit and herself, an insignificant girl wearing black woolen stockings and a shapeless jumper. For a moment this lifeless girl stands there, but then, slowly, she turns and in a way that is almost robotic starts moving away. Someone (Mme Freund perhaps?) picks up her coat and hands it to her—*Here, Eva, you'll need this*—and then, somehow, she's standing in front of the blond-haired man being handed her documents.

"Merci," she says automatically and drifts closer to the door, aching to look back at her mother—*just one last glimpse, is that too much to ask?* —but knowing that it's far too risky. Yet she can't bear to part this way. It's so heartless, so cold. But what choice does she have? *Maman, I love you, I do!* she whispers, willing her mother to somehow hear this secret farewell as she, Eva, steps through the door and enters a stairwell so narrow and dark it feels like a tunnel.

6 o'clock in the evening

Convinced that no one else will be coming in, Obersturmführer Barbie walks over to the switchboard operator and tells her to join the people in the back room. After that, anyone who calls will be greeted by one of his men saying, *"Es ist fertig mit diesen Leuten."* It's all over with those people.

Then the men are called. The Boches are polite—*Form groups of twelve, but hurry, please, your transport is waiting* —and the men get up. With a collective sigh of relief, they stretch themselves, exchange looks, hope for the best.

Rach Szulkapler, brother-less now, finds himself in the first group along with Dr Lanzenberg and Paul Guérin, the furrier's apprentice who smells of death. The Taubmanns, father and son, go into the third group along with Jacques Peskind, the Latvian news peddler, while Maier Weissman and André Deutsch are put in the next-to-the-last group.

Counting them a final time, the Germans discover they're one short. But then an old man, the kind who's almost never seen anymore, with side locks and a long fuzzy beard, is found praying in a corner of the back room. One of Klaus's men goes to pry him away, and he doesn't resist, only looks around and blinks his rheumy eyes in wonderment.

* * *

Victor Szulkapler is watching from a darkened doorway across from Number 12 when the first of the men emerge. Catching sight of Rachmil, he thinks his brother looks stronger and healthier than the others. At least he has a little meat on his bones. And he's better prepared, too, the only one with a decent pair of boots.

If only he'd been a little more adept, thinks Victor, and worked on his French and gotten himself a proper ID, but, no, Rach was the older brother who always had to know best. It was maddening . . . But, still, what will Victor do without him? Just look at him, will you, the way he leaps into the back of the truck: it's magnificent, almost beyond belief, an unforgettable feat that leaves Victor so shaken he can hardly breathe.

* * *

There are still two groups of men waiting to be led down the steps when sixteen-year-old Lea Katz finally comprehends that she's going to be taken away. Somehow, she'd talked herself into believing that they'd release the women, or at least anyone like herself who is under eighteen, but she sees now that there are no distinctions. Already, the Boches are nudging the women into line, telling them to gather up their things so they'll be ready.

Lea, dizzy with fear, looks around for the guy who called her "kitten"—he thought she was pretty, didn't he?—but the man is nowhere to be seen. She spots his boss, though, the one in the pinstriped suit, and quickly goes over to him.

"My mother is very sick, so I've got to go home tonight because there's no one else to take care of her," she tells him in a torrent of French. He doesn't respond, though, and so she adds, "Tomorrow morning, I'll go wherever you want me to, I promise, but tonight—"

He interrupts her then, saying in German that he hasn't understood a word she's said. It's a lie, though, and Lea knows it because she's heard him speaking French, but of course she can't say that. Instead, she grabs him by the elbow and repeats everything she'd said before, except this time in German.

For a moment he seems dumbfounded. But then he looks down at her hand on his elbow and his face darkens.

"*Das Freche dings vas du bist,*" he says—you insolent little thing—barking it out so loudly that the room falls silent. "When you came in here, you pretended you didn't know German." She shakes her head at this, but he continues: "No, I saw you. Koth was speaking German to you, but you spoke French back to him." He gives her a venomous look. "But you speak it well enough when you want to beg, don't you?" And then without warning, he raises his hand and slaps her hard, once on each cheek, so that she's spun one way and then the other. She staggers backward, expecting to be hit again, but then, just like that, his manner changes.

"You may go," he tells her calmly. "Just find your pocket-book and bring it to me." Lea doesn't understand, but she digs through the mound of discarded bags until she comes to the little red purse her mother gave her on her last birthday. She hands it to him, then watches as he extracts a couple of stamps. "Use these for the streetcar," he tells her. "Then come to the hôtel Terminus tomorrow and I'll give you back your bag and ID." He pauses, then adds, as if she didn't already know, "It's where the SD is."

She nods dumbly, ready to promise anything, when he adds, apropos of nothing, "We're going to let all of you go anyway."

It is an extraordinary statement, but she doesn't contradict it. She's ready to believe anything, anything at all, if only it will help her get out of here. But if he thinks she's going to present herself at the hôtel Terminus tomorrow, he's deluded. Because the only place she'll be tomorrow is at the *salon de coiffure* having her red hair dyed black.

Jacqueline Rozenfarb, who has watched all of this, studies the pinstriped man from the corner of her eye. She's afraid of him, of course, but he let the redheaded girl go, didn't he? So maybe he'd let her go too. But how can she approach him? And even if she did, what would she say? She pictures herself standing in front of him like a ninny, just waiting to be slapped.

But then the Boche—the hideous one, the one with the long yellow teeth—kicks her hard in the rear. "Get into line, will you?" he growls, and she looks around, realizing that there are only a couple of dozen people left, all of them women. In other words, just two groups. That's how close the end is. And she knows that if she does nothing, she'll be swept up along with the rest of them and taken to one of those horrible camps where her mother will never be able to find her. She peeks at the *chef* again, and determining that there's no other way, she braces herself to go up to him. But then she spots Gilberte Jacob, the social worker who'd helped her before, and runs over to her instead.

"Please, Gilberte, help me," she pleads. "I'm only fourteen and my mother's at home, waiting for me. I can't let them . . . I mean, the only reason I came here was to meet Chana . . . you know who I mean, the one with the baby. Otherwise, I wouldn't even be here."

Gilberte takes a deep breath. She cannot approach the *chef,* not after their previous exchange, but perhaps she could try that tall blond-headed man, the one who seems more or less reasonable. "All right," she says, "I'll see what I can do."

Quickly, she walks over to the desk where he's sorting ID cards into piles. *"S'il vous plait, monsieur,"* she says, addressing him as she might a *gendarme,* "but I need your assistance."

He only glares at her, though. *"Geh fort,"* he barks. *"Kannst du nicht sehen, das ich beschattigt bin?"* Gilberte understands only enough German to know that he's dismissing her, but the shove he gives her is unambiguous. Though not hard enough to knock her over, it still makes her stagger. "Go on, get into line with the others," he adds in French, gesturing toward the other, more obedient women who are waiting quietly by the door.

Gilberte is stunned. She starts to back away—the cause is probably hopeless anyway—but then a surge of anger goes through her, galvanizing her. "No, you don't understand. This isn't for me, it's for her," she says, turning to wave Jacqueline over. But the girl, half-hidden behind a bank of file cabinets, appears petrified. "C'mon, Jacqueline, don't waste this man's time," she says sharply, so sharply that Jacqueline scurries over. Gilberte takes a quick look at the Boche (amazingly, there's an expression of detached amusement on his face) and pushes Jacqueline forward. "You see," she says, trying to modulate her voice, "*cette petite* isn't even fifteen, and besides she is French. It's only by chance that she ended up here. She just dropped by to meet a friend."

The German looks closely at Gilberte and then at Jacqueline, who, though small to begin with, seems to shrink even more under his gaze. "Wait, I'll talk to the *chef*," he says, then crosses the room to intercept him.

Gilberte, who watches as the two men converse, thinks they look rather comical standing side by side: one tall, a natural *soldat*, a warrior, if you will; the other, in spite of his fancy suit, short and faintly absurd—a natural *tyranneau*. But as soon as she thinks this, she looks down at the floor for fear they'll see her face and know what she's thinking.

Jacqueline says nothing as they wait, but Gilberte, who is holding the little girl's hand, can feel her quivering. Soon, however, their intermediary is back. "*Libre*," he says simply and hands over Jacqueline's ID.

Jacqueline is overcome. She can go home, she'll see her mother again, she'll even be able to finish her class. The other women quickly gather around her, caressing and kissing her as they beg her to tell their families what's happened. She promises them that, yes, she'll do her best, but it isn't easy escaping from them. Finally, though, she extracts herself and pushes her way to the door, where she stops to look back at Gilberte.

In that moment, Gilberte, who's a professional, a trained social worker, forces herself to smile. But beneath the smile, a dark shard of resentment cuts through her: *Why is she always the one who has to save others? Why can't someone save her instead?*

At the end of the day

As soon as the women are loaded, the two canvas-topped lorries pull away from the curb in front of Number 12 rue Sainte-Catherine and head south toward the tip of the Presqu'île, that long peninsular finger dividing the Saône from the Rhône.

Maier Weissman, who sits near the back of the lead truck, watches as the familiar streets pass by, his thirsty eyes soaking up whatever they chance upon: news vendors hawking their papers, last-minute shoppers rushing to get home, storekeepers rolling up their awnings for the night. Then suddenly the Gare de Perrache lurches into view and Maier realizes that they're on his street, actually passing in front of his building. Eagerly, he looks up at his third-floor apartment, hoping for a last glimpse—Mariam holding up her birthday cake, Sylvie blowing him a kiss, little Ezekiel waving and grinning—but the window is dark. It's the blackout blinds, of course. How could he have forgotten about them? It's a small comfort, he supposes, to know his family is there on the other side of them, like players on a stage who are hidden from the audience, but knowing, as he does now, that he'll never see them again, not even from a distance, is devastating—a crushing pain that he feels right in the center of chest, which is heartbreak, yes, but also a very real attack of angina.

Soon, however, the Perrache is left behind and the Rhône comes into view. It is here that the drivers gun their engines, barreling across pont Gallieni and onto avenue Bertholet, a broad thoroughfare where people huddle at bus stops, stamping their feet and watching for a bus that may or may not arrive.

Eva Gottlieb is there, too, in a flat facing the street, so close in fact that, if only she'd known, she could have leaned out a window and yelled to her mother as she passed. But Eva, who's as far away from the window as she can get, is curled up in a fetal position on a bed that doesn't belong to her, or to Jacques either. He hovers over her, rubbing her back, whispering into her ear, telling her, over and over, that he'll be her mother, her father, her brother, whatever she needs him to be, but the words, though she hears them, aren't really words, just sounds strung together. She stares at the wall in front of her and then at the bedside table, empty except for a blue-and-white tin of Pastilles Vichy. Idly, she pries off the lid with her fingernail and examines the little white mints inside which seem so pointless and sad. Because who can eat candy now?

Certainly not her. Even thinking about it is an abomination.

In the meantime, only a little east of her, the lorries turn into Fort Lamothe, a military compound that's been taken over by the Wehrmacht. The trucks make their way through the heavy iron gates, then pull up in front of the barracks where an officer is waiting to take delivery. The driver of the lead truck jumps down and confers with him briefly before handing over the paperwork.

According to this manifest, there are eighty-six prisoners in all, sixty-two of them men and twenty-four women, including:

Five between the ages of thirteen and twenty,

Eight between twenty and thirty,

Twenty-one between thirty and forty,

Thirty between forty and fifty,

Thirteen between fifty and sixty,

Eight between sixty and seventy, and

One between seventy and eighty.

Among them, there are:

Twenty-two Poles,

Fourteen persons who consider themselves French but are disavowed by Vichy,

Twelve Austrians,

Four Germans,
Four Czechs,
Three Hungarians,
Three Romanians,
Two Russians,
One Latvian,
Six stateless persons, and
One *indéterminé*.

After a careful study of this paperwork and a final bit of discussion (the SD does not really trust the Wehrmacht), the prisoners are finally ordered out of the trucks. Shivering a little in the icy air, they shake off their stiffness, then look around, first at the stony walls before them and then at the blank sky overhead. No one says anything, but each of them is searching for the same thing: a single star, just one, which can offer them some small measure of hope.

Sadly, though, the clouds are so thick and low that their mass is impenetrable, even by stars.

COLLABORATION

Klaus lay next to Marianne in her big bed, watching the play of shadows on the ceiling and feeling vaguely out of sorts. He'd met Marianne at the end of 1942 when she'd barged into his office wearing a full-length mink and demanding a pass to visit her sister in Paris. She was older than Klaus by a good ten or fifteen years, but she wasn't bad looking (French women of her class never were), so when she invited him for dinner, he accepted without knowing quite what to expect. The meal had been excellent, though, and what followed was even better. In fact, she'd shown him a very good time. But that was six months ago, and the enthusiasm she'd exhibited then had pretty much worn off. Take tonight, for instance. Things had gotten off to a good start with the roast goose and a very nice Châteauneuf-du-Pape. But as for the rest of the evening—well, it had fallen short of what he'd hoped for. She just hadn't lived up to her end of the bargain. Peevishly, he glanced over at her and said, "You don't respond much, do you, Marianne?"

"*Comment?*" she asked sleepily, lifting her head from the pillow. "Did you say something?"

"I said you don't respond much anymore."

Marianne was taken aback. She'd heard him quite clearly the first time, but she'd been generous enough to pretend that she hadn't. She'd given him a chance to rescind what he'd said, or at least rephrase it. But what had he done? He'd repeated it almost verbatim. It was maddening, especially after everything she'd done for him. The cooking alone would have felled a less desperate woman.

But that was Klaus for you. France might be starving, but he couldn't do without his five-course meal. It was part of their deal. He sent her the food (ridiculous amounts of it, including eggs, butter, poultry, produce, seafood, anything you could imagine—even beef and chocolate) while she struggled alone in her kitchen to meet his culinary demands. This time he'd asked for roast goose stuffed with prunes and foie gras (it was a classic, he'd told her, as if she didn't know), and so she'd spent all day pitting prunes, mincing goose liver, then basting and turning her nine-pound bird until it was as glossy and brown as mahogany. By the time she set her tribute before him, she was almost too exhausted to eat. But was he happy? No, he wanted ardor too.

"Careful, Klaus," she told him, trying to keep the edge out of her voice. "I'm not one of your little *cocottes*, you know."

"Apparently not," he said. "They actually manage to muster a little passion."

Marianne lay back and looked around in an attempt to take comfort from her surroundings: the finely carved bedroom suite, the delicate pieces of Limoges, the stuccowork angels some long-ago plasterer had molded over the mirror. It didn't matter what Herr Obersturmführer thought. How could it? He was an arrogant little pup, a boor, an occupier—in other words, a Boche. It rendered his opinion irrelevant. Yet she'd done so many nice things for him, things that would have made her gag only a few months ago. That bath, for instance: soaping the blue-veined penis, dragging a washcloth through the cleft of his buttocks, then wiping him with a towel, all the way down to his toes, careful to dry between each one, on her knees while she did it, a big Turkish towel in her hands, perversely intent on humiliating herself.

The *maîtresse de maison* being retrained for geisha service.

"Oh, for goodness sakes, Klaus, don't be so naïve," she said. "Those girls are supposed to show you a good time. It's a performance, that's all."

Beside her, Klaus grunted. He wasn't going to waste his breath by responding, but honestly, what a lot of *Quatsch*. And the tone of her voice, did she really think she could get away with that—with *him*? He wondered if she had forgotten who he was: not just another lieutenant, but the *chef*, the man who kept order here in Lyon. If she didn't remember, well, others certainly did. All he had to do was walk through the streets to see a path clear in front of him. Even without his dog, Wolf, even without his uniform, the Lyonnais knew who he was and got out of his way.

Absently, Klaus glanced around the room, its every surface crowded with knick-knacks, and wondered how her husband, the captain, managed to sleep in it. Well, perhaps he was blind as well as impotent. But at least the man was alive and well, which might not have been the case if he, Klaus, hadn't made sure that the captain's name was removed from the *gendarmarie's* card file. But if Marianne wanted him to, if that really was her preference, he could easily have the card put back.

"Perhaps you're no longer satisfied with our arrangement?" he suggested, letting a certain implication leak into his voice. He sat up and swung his legs over the edge of the bed, then added: "I don't even know what I'm doing here. A woman your age. It's ridiculous."

Marianne, left to stare at his back, felt a numbness at the base of her spine. She was a fool, that's what she was. Her husband, a Jew, could be deported at any moment, and she was busy defending herself against what—a complaint so shallow that every married woman had probably heard it at one time or another?

"No, Klaus, don't say that," she said, sitting up and throwing her arms around his neck from behind. "You know how dull my life is. Except for your visits, what else do I have to look forward to?"

Klaus, hearing the panic in her voice, permitted himself a small smile. As threats go, his had been a modest one, but all the same it had worked. He decided to wait a bit, just to see what she would do.

But Marianne wasn't fazed by this strategy. Long years of living with her husband had taught her to deal with silences. Édouard simply wasn't the type to yell or engage in scenes. No, his pattern was to withdraw. This made it easy for her whenever Klaus was scheduled to visit. All she had to do was tell Édouard that the Milice was out looking for Jews, and he'd retreat to the countryside.

Just wait for a little, she told herself, watching as a moist April breeze pushed the crocheted curtains into the room. It wasn't hard to figure out what Klaus was doing. He was punishing her, putting her in her place, reminding her that he had the upper hand. And the worst part was that he did. She thought of M. Adelman, the German Jew with the dry goods store who'd been led away early one morning by a pair of *gendarmes*. By now, he was probably in Rivesaltes or one of those other detention camps. But Édouard was French and had served in the *La Grande Guerre*—had even lost an arm to it—so that made a difference. Or did it? Everything was so confusing these days, so topsy-turvy.

She pressed her cheek to Klaus's bare back, which was warm, almost hot, and thinly coated with sweat. "Don't leave," she whispered, tasting the saltiness of his skin. "I couldn't stand it if you did. It would be . . ." But she didn't know what it would be. Better just to direct her lips to the nape of his neck with its short, bristly hairs, then shift around to nibble on the lobe of his right ear (so strange the way it turned out, just like a little handle).

Klaus, caught off guard by the deftness of her strategy, barked out a laugh. He'd been prepared for what—tears, angst, abject apologies—and here she was biting his ear instead. Men were always saying what a mystery women were, but mostly they weren't. Marianne, though, was different. He never knew quite what to expect from her. She kept him guessing, always mixing surrender with defiance. She reminded him of a child clamoring to be picked up, but then wriggling to get away.

He swung his legs back onto the bed and propped himself against the headboard with pillows. "C'mere, *ma chérie*," he said, patting the spot next to him. He really hadn't meant to fight with her, but she'd pushed him into it with that passive routine of hers. Still, as women went, or at least the women he knew, she was probably the easiest, the plushest, the most comfortable of them all. But why, he wondered, had she called him naïve? He hadn't liked that.

In his younger years, it was true, he'd missed out on a lot, but now it was different. Now all the prettiest girls in Lyon put themselves in his way, laughing cluelessly at whatever he said, brushing up against him if they could, sometimes leaving folded scraps of paper inscribed with their phone numbers. He supposed some of them weren't much better than *putains,* just out for what they could get, but others were really very sweet.

Take Mimiche, for instance: All he had to do was walk into Le Lapin Blanche and look at her small feline face to see how much she wanted him, right then, that very moment. But it was never that simple. He had to wait around until she was done for the evening, then woo her with a late dinner and plenty of wine (yes, plenty of that) and maybe even some cognac later on. The rest of it was good, though, because she did moan, she did writhe, and there were even times when she cried out. But did she even know whose bed she was in? He wasn't sure.

"Tell me something, will you, Marianne," he said, trying to sound casual. "Just what did you mean when you said it was all a performance?"

Marianne was incredulous. "Well, I think it's obvious, don't you?" But no sooner had she said it than she reconsidered: perhaps it wasn't obvious to *him*. Klaus gave himself such airs, with his impeccable table manners and courtly reserve (ridiculous in a thirty-year-old), but she knew it was only posturing. She could see for herself how self-conscious he was, how much he depended on her for admiration and respect.

Klaus looked at her and frowned. "That's not very helpful," he said, irritated by her evasiveness. "Can't you just answer the question?"

Something in the tone of his voice flustered Marianne. She knew she ought to say something but could think of nothing.

Klaus gave her a hard tight look. "You need to tell me," he said. "When I ask a question, you need to answer."

Marianne felt her body stiffen. He hadn't raised his voice, in fact he'd lowered it, but it was suddenly stark, hollow, pitiless —almost like a voice from the grave. And then it came to her: this must be his interrogation voice, the voice that the "Butcher of Lyon" used on his prisoners.

"I really shouldn't have used the word 'performance,'" she said hastily, "because it's not that simple. I mean, who knows?

Women react differently." It was raining now, and she paused for a moment to listen to the soft patter of raindrops on her flowerbeds. "But you must know that women pretend." She faltered. "Sometimes, I mean. It happens."

Klaus absorbed this quietly. He'd heard of it of course, but had never thought of it in connection with himself. Women might fake an orgasm with others, but with him? The idea was inconceivable. "But you'd never do anything like that, would you, Marianne?"

She forced herself to meet his eyes. "No, of course not. Never with you." It was a lie. Of course she'd pretended, over and over again, especially at the beginning, but it would be folly to admit that now.

For several moments Klaus said nothing and she worried that he might not believe her, but then he reached out and pulled her into his shoulder. "That's good," he said, giving her an affectionate squeeze, "because I want to be able to trust you." She expected him to go on from there, extolling the importance of trust in a relationship like theirs, but instead he turned away and started searching the top of the nightstand with his free hand. "You haven't seen my cigarettes, have you?" he asked.

"Your cigarettes?" she asked, glancing at the table. "Oh, I don't know. Behind the shepherdess maybe?"

"The what?"

"See that little figurine," she said, pointing to a china statuette of a girl wearing numerous petticoats and carrying a staff.

"That's what this is? A shepherdess?" asked Klaus, picking up the hollow figurine and examining it skeptically. In his estimation, this so-called shepherdess (who looked more like Marie Antoinette than a peasant) was far too dainty to be associated with livestock of any kind, even poultry. But that was Limoges for you: so fragile you hardly dared breathe on it. It was also rather like France, he thought, setting the figurine down and reaching for his pack of cigarettes—decorative on the outside, but with nothing solid underneath.

Klaus tapped out a cigarette and lit it, then took a long, luxurious drag. He was in a better mood now, more relaxed.

"I hope I didn't offend you," he said.

"Offend me?" asked Marianne, surprised at this shift in mood.

"Earlier, I mean. When I said that you were . . . well, you know . . ."

"You mean when you said that I was frigid?"

Klaus gave a small shrug. "I didn't say you were frigid, just not very responsive." Then, as if warming to his subject, he added: "They're not the same thing, you know. Frigid is never being able to respond. But unresponsive, that's more of a choice. It's choosing to be temporarily frigid."

Marianne nearly laughed out loud. The circular reasoning was one thing, but the ponderous tone? Perfect, maybe, for a meeting of *Jungvolk*, but ludicrous when directed toward a woman who catered to his every whim, who entertained him lavishly—and who was here with him, at this very moment, in the post-coital bed.

"You make it sound simple," she said.

He blew a stream of smoke toward the ceiling. "Well, it is, isn't it?"

"I guess so. For men anyway, but for women it's a little different."

Klaus looked over at her. "How do you mean?"

Marianne hesitated, uneasy about the turn their conversation was taking. "Well, I guess you could say that it's not quite so straightforward,"

Klaus thought about this for a moment. He wasn't sure what she meant, but he had an idea. "Do you mean that it's harder for a woman to get into the mood? Is that it?" he asked, putting out his cigarette in one of Marianne's fussy little ashtrays.

"Well, maybe, I'm not really sure . . . but, yes, something like that I suppose."

Klaus nodded because this was something he'd noticed himself. Nature seemed to have put men and women on different levels, and it was only through a lot of maneuvering on the man's part—a surfeit of wine, an endless litany of compliments, perhaps even a gift or two—that the gap could be bridged. He supposed it was like that throughout the animal kingdom: the eager buck having to compensate for the shy doe. But it still seemed contradictory to him, unnecessary, a waste of everyone's time. "It does complicate things," he said. "All that wining and dining and—"

"No, that's not what I mean," said Marianne. "Not that those things aren't nice," she added quickly. "They are, and a woman always appreciates a certain amount of romance, but there are other kinds of attention . . ." She felt her face heating up and looked away. This was intolerable. How could she be talking about something like this with a Nazi *bourreau*?

Beside her, Klaus cleared his throat. "I've heard there's a special way of . . . a certain part of the anatomy that's very sensi—"

"Sorry," she said, sitting up all the way and hugging her knees. "I can't talk about this anymore. It's impossible." She looked around the room, taking in the plaster angels, the dainty writing desk with its little drawers, the dresser that—but here she stopped, startled by the sight of something heavy and metallic next to her perfume bottles. She stared at it for a moment before realizing it was Klaus's revolver. He must have left it there when he was undressing. It lay there, quiet and still, like a secret threat, a reminder, if she needed one, that he held Édouard's life in his hands.

"Would you like me to put that somewhere else?" asked Klaus, who'd been watching her.

She nodded (*Yes, please, take it away, throw it out the window, bury in the backyard, whatever, just get rid of it*), then pressed her forehead to her knees so she wouldn't have to see him walking around her bedroom with a gun in his hand. She could hear him, though, padding across the room to get the pistol, then walking back with it and putting it somewhere— just where, she wasn't sure, probably with the clothes he'd draped over her desk chair. Not until the bed springs squeaked, protesting his weight as he got back into bed, did she look up.

"Thank you," she said, lying down again. "It's silly, I know, but it seemed to be pointing right at me."

He nodded, acknowledging her discomfort (even though, secretly, he found himself savoring it). "I don't suppose Édouard ever brings home anything like that, does he?"

She shook her head. "No, never." The thought was inconceivable. Édouard didn't even like to hunt quail. "But how did you know I was thinking about Édouard?"

Klaus laughed good-naturedly and propped himself up on his elbow. "*Eh bien*, Marianne, I'm a psychic, didn't I tell you? It's one of my lesser-known talents."

This was the side of Klaus, beaming and genial, that emerged every now and again, showing its feathers and then disappearing into the treetops again. It always took her by surprise how he could cheer up this way, even make fun of himself. But it posed a problem for her because then, for a moment or two, she'd find herself liking him. Or maybe not liking him exactly—because how could she, he was the Gestapo —but somehow becoming more fully aware of him: the firm belly and nice head of hair, the boyish grin that framed his thirty-two perfect teeth (yes! perfect). Even his heavily accented French had grown on her, becoming at times almost endearing. No, she thought, sleeping with him wasn't a betrayal of her husband (not really, only a means to an end), but all the rest of it was: enjoying his company, soaking up his presence, liking his hard clean smell—wanting more from him than was decent.

"Do you know," she said, staring up at the ceiling, "I've never had a conversation with Édouard like the one we were just having." She paused. "About sex, I mean."

"No? Never?"

She felt the need to defend herself. "You have to understand how young I was when I married Édouard. Barely eighteen. And I'd been in a convent school so I was completely ignorant." She paused. "Well, all girls were then," she added, shaking her head in retrospective disbelief. "And then later, after the war, Édouard was too . . . well, fragile. It wasn't just the arm, but shell shock too. At any rate, he was . . . well, just not the same."

Gazing down at her, Klaus pushed the hair off her forehead so he could see her widow's peak, which for some reason intrigued him. "It was like that with my father, too," he ventured. "I don't know what he was like before the war. My mother married him so she must have thought . . . well, I guess he must have been all right, but then when he came home from the war he had this terrible wound in his neck"—here Klaus clutched the side of his own neck—"and it was . . ."

"I'm not sure why, but for some reason they couldn't remove the shrapnel, so it never healed."

"Ouch," said Marianne, grimacing. "That must have been painful."

"Something tormented him anyway. And then . . . well, he

started drinking . . . and after that, it was . . . you know . . ." His voice trailed off and he looked away.

Marianne waited a moment, processing what he had said, what he had suggested. "He tormented you too, didn't he?" she asked.

Klaus did not respond, but a look came over his face—resigned, wary, ashamed—which she had never seen before.

She reached out to touch his cheek and was about to say something else, but almost instantly his face changed, and the mask snapped back into place. "You have to understand, he was an honorable man," he said. "That wound of his was a badge of honor."

Silence fell over the room then, leaving only the drowsy sound of the rain, the muted whistle of a train (probably the overnight express to Paris).

"There's a little wine left over from dinner," said Marianne, getting up and reaching for her peignoir. "It would be a shame to let it go to waste." Marianne had no children, but in moments like this, she thought she would have made a good mother, that parenting would have come to her naturally.

When she returned with the wine, he was leaning against the headboard smoking another cigarette. "If you wouldn't mind, light one of those for me, would you?" she said, setting his glass on the nightstand next to him.

He pulled a cigarette from the pack and handed it to her, then waited until she'd climbed onto her side of the bed to reach over and light it for her.

Marianne smiled her thanks and inhaled deeply, holding the smoke in her lungs for a moment or two before exhaling. It was a lovely evening, tranquil and warm, so warm that she hadn't wanted to close the window when it started raining. Even now, the breeze felt good, delicate and frilly . . .

"You seem to be in a good mood," Klaus observed as she sipped her wine.

"Mmm," she murmured, thinking that this was the perfect way to end the evening: with a glass of wine, a cigarette. It was civilized, dignified. It brought things to a natural conclusion. Their arrangement was supposed to be straightforward, a simple quid pro quo, but it wasn't. All evening long, she'd been back and forth: resenting him one moment, then relishing him the next; wishing he'd leave, then hoping he'd stay. She was tired now and wanted her house back.

Klaus slipped an arm around her and kissed the top of her head. "You were going to tell me about women, remember— what they like, what makes them happy."

She dropped the stub of her cigarette into the puddle of wine that was left in her glass and set it on the nightstand. "Why don't we save that for another time. It's late and you have to get up in the morning. And besides," she added, "I'm tired."

"So you're not going to tell me?" he asked, putting out his cigarette. His tone was boyish and coaxing.

She sighed. "Seriously, Klaus, it's just too big a topic. I should never have brought it up."

"But you did," he said, reaching under her peignoir and rolling his thumb over her nipple.

Marianne was surprised. She hadn't realized that he'd been paying any attention to her at all, to what she liked, what she didn't.

But it was too distracting. She stopped him with her hand and tried to think. She needed to keep some small part of herself intact and away from him. After all, she was a sovereign being, there was no need for her to capitulate at every turn. He might want to know about the secrets of the female body, but she wanted to clean up the kitchen and take a bath of her own.

"But Édouard . . ." she said weakly, offering up his name as an excuse.

"What about him?" asked Klaus, nuzzling the side of her neck. "You know Édouard can't satisfy you. He'd like to but he can't. He's too old and weak. And besides, he's running for his life."

It was true, everything he said was true, but she couldn't bear to hear it. "Don't say that," she said.

"I know," he said quickly, "and nothing is going to happen to him. I'll see to that. You have my word as a German officer."

Inwardly, Marianne flinched. A German officer? Why would he say that? Did he think she needed reminding? But of course that was it, the crux of their evil compact. If he had been anyone else, he would never have entered her house, much less her bedroom. But the war had boxed her in. For as long as Édouard needed her protection, she was determined to go on with this "affair." But how long would that be? There was talk that the Allies might stage an invasion this spring. But nothing was certain. Even after Stalingrad, it was still quite possible that the Germans would win.

But in any case, she was stuck for the duration. So why not enjoy herself a little? Let Klaus cater to her for a change.

She turned to look into his face. In the darkness, his eyes seemed very large, the pupils soaking up all but a narrow rim of the pale blue surrounding them.

"You're right," she said finally. "There *is* a spot that's very sensitive, very—"

"Show me," he said, kissing the top of her shoulder.

She hesitated, remembering herself as a child at the end of a pier, ready to jump in but wondering how cold the water would be, how deep, how muddy. But she'd come this far, there was no turning back now. "Yes, all right," she said, "but you have to promise to do what I say."

"Whatever *madame* commands," said Klaus in a mock-serious voice.

"Good," she said shortly, all business now as she shrugged off her peignoir and lay back on the bed. Next, she had him prop up her hips with pillows, then parted her thighs to make room for him there. When he had repositioned himself—"*D'accord*, that's good," she said, encouraging him—she directed him to a spot just below the crest of her pubic bone. "This is where you want to be," she told him.

"Indeed," said Klaus, fitting his hand to the cleft that always reminded him of a thickly padded envelope and letting his fingers drift downward.

"No, not there. Higher up," said Marianne, placing her hand on his and guiding it upward. "There's a button there," she explained, seeing the confusion on his face. "Well, not a button exactly, but you'll feel it. Just keep looking."

Klaus had no idea what she was talking about—she really wasn't helping him much—but then he thought about how Mimiche, and in fact all women, were in possession of the same "button," and recommitted himself to seeking it out, until—suddenly—he heard her suck in her breath.

"Klaus, not so hard," she said.

"I'm hurting you?"

"A little," she said, then quickly added: "But don't stop. Just not so hard."

He was becoming more and more frustrated. Really, he had hurt her? It was hard to believe, but perhaps she was trying to humiliate him, to make him look like a fool. The French were like that sometimes, stepping on your foot in the Métro if they could, then pretending it was just an accident. But he was determined to discover this secret, so he lightened his touch as much as possible.

Marianne half-lifted her head. "You just need to be a little more—" But then she saw the look on his face—clearly, he was losing patience—and felt a stab of anxiety. If this little exercise of theirs failed, she could only imagine the retaliation he'd mete out. "Wait, why don't I just show you?" she said, taking his hand and redirecting it where she wanted it to go.

"That's it?" said Klaus, touching the tiny protrusion, then massaging it gently.

"Am I doing it right? I'm not hurting you, am I?"

"*Non, pas du tout,*" she murmured, sounding dazed. "*C'est parfait.*"

Relieved, Klaus continued his ministrations. He wasn't sure what he'd expected, but he was still surprised at the way she lay there so completely still she was practically motionless. It was an *active* stillness, though, as if she'd gone deep inside herself, so deep that any abruptness on his part was liable to break the spell.

What Klaus didn't know was that she was waiting. Marianne was not going to ask, she was not going to plead—at least not with words—but as she felt the tension building within her she grew impatient. Raising her hips, she very deliberately tipped them in his direction. She even moaned a little. It was not an act, everything she expressed was something she *felt*, but she wanted him to understand that she needed more, that he hadn't gone quite far enough.

Klaus paused, confused by the sudden change in her, but delighted with the response he'd elicited. He touched the tip again, now swollen and more accessible, and fondled it lightly. At first, nothing, and then a murmur. Later, a rotation that seemed to come from the core of her body. And then, all at once, a quick lifting of her hips as though she were presenting herself to him, inviting him in, urging him, begging. A simple response then to bring his mouth down to her, to enclose the small button with his tongue and coax it still further.

Poised for exactly this, her body reacted with a cascade of

concentric undulations that gradually mellowed to an all-encompassing feeling of bliss. Suddenly, the world was a very good place and she loved everyone in it. She would have forgotten all about Klaus if he hadn't quizzed her from the foot of the bed: "Was that good? Did you like it?"

"*Oui, très bon,*" she said, sounding delirious even to herself. And it was true, he'd shown her a very good time. But seeing him there, grinning up at her stupidly as he lay prostrate before her was even more satisfying. She had no idea how the war would end, but if this was the face of the enemy, then there was hope for France.

And for her? she wondered, gazing up at the little angels that fluttered above the mirror.

But they were vexed with her and turned away. She supposed it had been too much for them: her open legs, his open mouth, that terrible gun. *But, really, what harm had been done? Even if she'd loved him for a moment, was that so awful? She was human after all, not some automaton.*

But then a damp breeze came in through the window, and she felt the wetness on her cheeks. She was crying? Really? But how could that be? She never cried. And those muffled sobs, where were they coming from? Could it be the angels? *But why would they be weeping? They understood her motives, how pure they were, and that underneath, in her innermost being, she was a good woman, a good wife.*

But the angels had seen. They knew how completely she'd turned herself over to the Butcher of Lyon, how she'd succumbed to his attentions, how—even now, this very moment —she lay basking in the shameful afterglow of them. She'd bargained herself away— and not just her body this time, but the deepest, truest part of herself—and for what? A momentary sensation that was as hollow and raw as the crack of a jackboot on pavement.

THE MAKING OF A MARTYR

(1) Kaltenbrunner document

Reading SS-Obergruppenführer Dr. Ernst Kaltenbrunner's report dated June 29, 1943, we can tell, just from its turgid style, that he labored over it. Writing may not have come to him easily.

But the drinking didn't help either. Sitting there in his big Berlin office swilling champagne and French brandy from morning till night, he had a tendency to repeat himself, to become ponderous. Yet the report he produced is generally factual. In it, he says that the raid, which was carried out by Klaus Barbie of the SD in Lyon, France, took place a little after 3 P.M. on Monday, June 21 in Caluire, a nearby suburb. The report goes on to say that seven high-ranking resisters were arrested, but that "Max" was not among them—a fact which Kaltenbrunner attributes to his having "been arrested in a French police raid."

As it turns out, Kaltenbrunner wasn't wrong about the time, or the place, or the number of men taken into custody, but he was wrong about the mysterious "Max" because "Max" *was* there, scooped up along with all the others at Dr Dugoujon's three-story villa.

(2) Monday, June 21

It's relatively easy to imagine Obersturmführer Klaus Barbie returning to Lyon with his load of prisoners on that first day of summer in 1943. He's elated of course, and why shouldn't he be? These aren't your everyday couriers transporting small arms or leaflets from one rendezvous point to another, but high-echelon officers from de Gaulle's Secret Army.

Wasting no time, Klaus quickly separates those found in the upper room from those who were in the doctor's waiting room, and is just starting in on a man called Lassagne, when Stengritt bursts into his office, waving a fistful of documents and shouting, *"'Max' est parmi eux."* At first Barbie thinks he is joking—"Max?" "Max," de Gaulle's personal envoy? "Max," head of the French Resistance?—but Harry keeps nodding, an ear-to-ear grin splitting his big handsome mug. Klaus laughs out loud, unable to stop himself, because "Max" is like the pot of gold at the end of the rainbow, a prize so big, so outlandish, that his superiors will have no choice but to look up and take notice.

The telex from Knochen in Paris said, *"Sit tight, Kaltenbrunner's sending out a team,"* but why should he wait? Because he's merely a lieutenant? Because he doesn't have the same fancy degrees that Knochen does? Because he doesn't believe in molly-coddling prisoners?

Well, fuck them. They're as bad as his father who'd spent his short, miserable life hurling insults at Klaus—*You're worthless, inane, ridiculous . . . just an unfortunate accident, that's all.* And his grandfather had been just as bad, withholding the money

Klaus needed for university, money that should have gone to him after his father's death. But when Klaus asked for it, the old man had shoved him out the door as if he were some sort of imposter.

But they were wrong, both of them. And Klaus will prove it because no matter what anyone thinks he's good at his job. And he knows how to make people talk. It's like springing a lock: just apply the right pressure and almost anybody will open up.

(3) Montluc Prison

At Lyon's *Centre d'histoire* on avenue Berthelot—the very same building from which Barbie operated—we can see a page from the prison register dated June 21, 1943. On it are recorded the names of the men arrested that day in Caluire. All had been interrogated briefly, then sent on to Montluc at 11 P.M. where they were made to sign their names as if registering at a hotel:

> *Aubry, Henri, married, born 3 March 1911, Catholic,*
> *former reserve officer (cell 75);*
> *Dugoujon, Frédéric, bachelor, born 30 June 1913,*
> *Catholic, doctor (cell 129);*
> *Ermelin, Claude, bachelor, born 7 February 1912,*
> *Catholic, office worker (cell 77);*
> *Lacaze, Albert, married, born 21 May 1884, Protestant,*
> *artist (cell 69);*
> *Lassagne, Andre-Louis, bachelor, born 23 April 1911,*
> *Catholic, lycée teacher (cell 117);*
> *Martel, Jacques, bachelor, born 22 August 1897,*
> *Catholic, decorator (cell 130); and*
> *Schwartzfeld, Emile-Lucas, married, born 5 December*
> *1885, Catholic, engineer (cell 65).*

These are the seven resisters who fell into Barbie's clutches at Caluire—but, wait, wasn't there also an eighth man, and if so what happened to him? Isn't this something we need to look into?

(4) M. Cornu

Early the next morning—and we mean early, so early it's still dark—M. Cornu is awakened by someone pounding on his front door. Or is it several someones? He sits up in bed, hears the thick accents: *"German police. Open up."*

No! He thinks, it can't be, but he knows that it is. He fumbles his way into a dressing gown, flaps down the stairs in his slippers and pulls open the door. And there they are: big, well-nourished men wearing suits too expensive for anyone except the Gestapo.

He starts to say something, but they push their way past him, yelling, "Henri Aubry, where is his flat?"

Shaken, M. Cornu points to the staircase. *"Premier étage,"* he gasps. *"Sur la rue."* And they swarm up the stairs, leaving him barely able to breathe as he hears, first, Mme Raisin's protests and then her screams.

Later, after they've gone, M. Cornu creeps upstairs to see the damage for himself. In their search for documents, they'd upended furniture, cut open sofa cushions, sawn the legs off chairs. He stands in the center of the room and shakes his head. M. Aubry: such a nice man and so quiet, gone almost all of the time. And his secretary, poor Mme Raisin, did they have to remove her too? But he knows that the two of them must have been up to something, that they weren't as innocent as they pretended to be, and it makes him angry, the way they took advantage of him, exploiting his good nature, putting the whole house in danger.

But M. Cornu wouldn't feel this way if he knew what was happening to Aubry at that very moment. Beatings of course, needles under the fingernails, electrodes attached to testicles, a dislocation of the shoulder. They think he's "Max," that's why they're trying so hard. But, for the time being, it's useless because this guy is stubborn, he won't say a thing.

(5) *Photograph*

We are told by the Aubracs and other Resistance survivors that Barbie was a monster, the Butcher of Lyon, a sadist through and through. And yet, when we see his official SS portrait, he looks deceptively normal, in a way almost pleasant. Heinz Hollert, who was Barbie's onetime superior, looks cold, his face and eyes blank, and Erich Bartelmus, head of the Jewish Section under Barbie, looks fleshy and stupid, but Barbie himself, wearing a coat and tie, looks like a neighbor or somebody's nephew or a clerk in some government office.

And there's something about the eyes, too. Rudolph Pechel, founder of the *Deutsch Rundschau* once said, "All the SS men have this in common: cold eyes like those of fish, reflecting a complete absence of inner life, a complete lack of sentiments." And it's true, Bartelmus' eyes *are* fishy and so are Hollert's. But Barbie's are different. There's an uneasiness there, a sadness that is hard to explain. Or are we imagining things? Still, we know what his father was like—a drunkard, quick with his fists, savage when it came to Klaus—so, perhaps, what we're seeing is the residual despair of that long-ago child who was born three months too early—that is to say, three months before Anna, his mother, could convince Klaus Sr. to marry her.

Today, "illegitimate" is an almost meaningless word, but in 1913 it was a curse. You couldn't inherit and it was never forgotten. In villages like Udler, where the Barbies lived, some people even crossed the street to avoid meeting him. And nothing could ever erase the stigma. Even wearing a uniform of the Reich or one of the custom-made suits favored by the Gestapo, Klaus Barbie was still a lesser being.

(6) Dr Dugoujon

After his first night of captivity, Dr Dugoujon (who looks far too young to be a physician) stumbles into the prison courtyard carrying his bucket. Shuffling along behind the others, he dumps its contents into the drain and tries to think what day it is. Monday? No, that was yesterday. Tuesday then: it must be Tuesday. Perhaps, he thinks, trying to rally himself, he ought to start keeping track of the days on the wall of his cell, but how? He has no writing implement, and they've taken away his belt whose buckle, or the prong anyway, could have been used to scratch some sort of record onto the wall. He stares down at his shoes, remembering that at this time yesterday, he'd been sitting in his own dining room being served breakfast by his housekeeper...

But just at this moment his thoughts are interrupted by someone who slips into line beside him.

"Dr Dugoujon," the man says, his voice raspy and strained. "Please, lift your head."

Dugoujon looks up, recognizing him as one of the men who was arrested at his house the day before—Martel, perhaps. He is a little shorter than average (though only a little shorter than Dugoujon himself) and wears a white silk scarf wrapped around his throat. Later, Dugoujon will recall that scarf and think how odd it had seemed, how out of place in that grim setting.

"They kept asking me about 'Max,'" Dugoujon explains to Martel, "but I'd never heard of him." Then, as if excusing himself, he adds: "Really, I don't know anything. I was just a classmate of Lacaze. That's why the meeting was at my—"

But the white-scarfed figure puts up a hand to stop him. Obviously, he doesn't want to hear anymore. But he smiles as he backs away. *"Bon courage,"* he says, then melts into the crowd.

(7) Reward

That same morning, Barbie receives a message from Bartolet, a French police inspector, who says he's arrested a man named René Hardy. Surely this is of interest to the Gestapo because didn't someone escape from the Caluire dragnet just yesterday? Shots were fired, *n'est-ce pas?*

And this man was hit by a bullet, in fact the bone in his left forearm was shattered.

So come on, cough up, we want our usual reward. Twenty thousand francs, that's nothing for the Gestapo, just petty cash, that's all.

(This was the gist of this message, if not quite the phrasing.)

(8) Confession

On Wednesday morning, Raymond Aubrac, who is one of the Caluire seven (listed as Claude Ermelin on the register), sees Henri Aubry in the courtyard of the prison. He is bare to the waist and black from beatings.

"I've been beaten," he says. "I've talked."

And then, a little before noon, two Gestapo men come to get Jacques Martel from cell 130.

(9) Another photograph

He's about to become a martyr, this man who calls himself Martel. Within years, we'll see his name—his real name, that is —attached to streets, schools, plaques, shrines. His image, as iconic as General Pétain's once was, will be reproduced every-where: a youngish man, who leans against a wall wearing a dark overcoat and scarf, with his hat, a broad-brimmed trilby, pulled down low on his forehead—see, all the trappings of a spy.

But his face, sometimes described as looking like a tired adolescent's, is not a spy's face. Just look at the dark playful eyes, the lips that seem on the verge of widening into a smile. There is nothing suspicious about this man, nothing threatening.

But we know what happened to him, so that darkens our viewing of this photo. And then there's the scarf, which is worn not for warmth but to hide an ugly scar that stretches across his throat. It's a scar that dates back to the beginning of the war when he was still a *préfet* in Chartres and didn't yet know what the Germans were capable of.

(10) Cell 129

On Wednesday evening, Dr. Dugoujon looks out of the peephole in the iron-plated door of his cell and observes Martel being brought back for the night. His ankles keep giving way, turning inward so that he staggers every third or fourth step. If it weren't for his captors holding him up, he'd collapse. There's an ugly gash on his right temple, too. It's so deep Dugoujon can't imagine the implement that was used to inflict it—a hatchet perhaps?—but whatever it was, his face is a bloody mess.

Even more ominous, though, are the two men called in to guard him. Dugoujon isn't sure what this means, but he can tell that the Boches think this man is important—so important they don't want to take a chance on his committing suicide. It makes Dugoujon wonder: could this be "Max"? He decides then that it must be.

(11) Provence

Two months earlier, on the Monday after Easter, this same man (not yet bloodied, still in control of his legs and faculties) can be seen saying goodbye to his sister after a weekend in Saint-Andiol. He is on one side of the garden gate holding his bicycle while she stands on the other, feeling cut off from him.

"Laure, there's something I need to tell you," he says, his voice catching the way it always has since his "accident." "I'm attempting something very difficult right now. I can't tell you what it is, but if it works out, I'll be crossing the Channel to join de Gaulle."

"You mean London?" she asks as a nearby rooster crows raucously. Somehow, it hadn't occurred to her that he'd be leaving the country indefinitely.

"Max" smiles grimly. "*Oui*, I have to. They are getting closer every day."

"They? The French police or the Gestapo or . . ."

But he waves the question away. "Don't worry. I'm doubling my precautions. But you have to promise not to write to me. I'll send you a note from time to time. It will come by courier. But you can't write to me. Not even if *maman* is ill." He pauses. "Not even if she dies."

Laure opens her mouth to say something, but he stops her. "Laure, you can't. They'd arrest me at the funeral."

She sags against the gate then, her whole body going slack. Her brother had been a servant of the state—in fact, the youngest *préfet* ever appointed—but he could just as easily have been an artist. Hadn't he illustrated Tristan Corbière's poetry? Hadn't his satirical cartoons appeared in all sorts of magazines? But that was a lifetime ago. Now he's being hunted by the police, at risk of being arrested every time he steps into the street.

"It's hard, I know," says her brother, reaching across the gate to embrace her, "but you've got to promise."

"I'm just so scared," she says, clutching the cloth of his jacket. "If something happens, how will I . . . I mean, I just don't know what I'd do without . . ."

"*Ma chère* Laure," he says, lifting her head from his shoulder and holding her at arm's length, "you do everything without me now."

She shakes her head—there is nothing to say to this—and tries to squeeze back the tears she can feel forming. It is still early, but the sky is lightening. They both know that he needs to be on his way, yet they stand there a moment longer divided from each other by the pickets of the gate.

Finally, though, he leans forward and kisses her on both cheeks. "*À bientot, courage, je t'aime,*" he says, the words running together as if he can't get them out quickly enough. And then, all at once, he's mounted his bicycle and is on his way down the road.

She stands there, following him with her eyes as he moves

farther and farther away from her, watching until he is no more than an imaginary speck on the road to Avignon.

(12) Second interrogation

On Thursday, just like the evening before, Dr Dugoujon is watching from his prison peephole as "Max" is once more returned to his cell. Barely conscious, his head lolling like a doll's, he's half carried, half dragged by his two guards. A bandage wrapped around his head is soaked with blood, and his clothes hang in tatters. With each step forward, a harsh moan comes out of him.

"It's really a shame," Dugoujon hears one of the guards saying.

"But he's a dangerous man," replies the other.

(13) M. Rougis

There are always witnesses. That's one thing history teaches us. And Claude Rougis is one of them. As a council employee, he'd been sent to Caluire on June 21 to scrape out the gutters on either side of the road. So, he was there when one of the men being arrested at Dr Dugoujon's villa took off running. He zigzagged across place Castellane, then jumped a low wall and plunged into the woods leading down to the river. Shots were fired and one or two of the Germans even went after him, but their search was over almost before it began.

M. Rougis, who'd seen the man throw himself into a ditch full of nettles, couldn't imagine how he'd avoided detection. As he told a journalist years later with deadpan sarcasm, "The

Gestapo didn't think to look in the ditch among the grass and such. Funny, that."

(14) Third interrogation

We don't know exactly what happened on Friday, June 25 when "Max" was taken to Barbie's headquarters for his third confrontation with the Butcher, but it isn't hard, based on what other prisoners have said, to imagine the Obstuf pacing back and forth, casting an occasional glance at his prisoner who sits slumped on a chair in front of him. Mischker and Koth had spent the last couple of hours working him over and it shows. His face is the color of a ripe plum, one eye is swollen shut, and gouts of blood stain his shirtfront. But he's conscious, thinks Klaus as he pulls out his desk chair and sits down. He can answer questions if he wants to.

"Now, 'Max,'" he says quietly, folding his hands on top of the desk and pretending to have all the time in the world, "I know we've been hard on you, and you've held up admirably.

"But really, what is the point? Don't you think we already know all about your *Armée secrète?*"

Across from him, "Max" lifts his head and squints at his interrogator through his good eye, bracing himself for what he senses is coming . . . a friendly chat, benign, harmless, a respite . . . Except he knows that it won't be. You're tired . . . then they offer you something—a cigarette, some brandy, whatever—and it's hard, incredibly hard, to refuse. That's how small the space around you is . . . just the two of you . . . And everything's over anyway, so what does it matter. . . a sip of brandy for one or two small bits of information—letterboxes already burnt, agents already arrested? But then, after that, it's too easy . . . and he's weak . . . It's like the time before, in Chartres . . .

"After all, no one can be expected to hold out forever," continues Klaus, trying to keep the vexation out of his voice. But it's not easy. Knochen has been on his ass all week, and the telex he sent today made it clear: all seven of the Caluire prisoners need to be turned over to BDS Paris by tomorrow at the latest.

Klaus doesn't think they'll be able to do much better than he has, but they can try. What's the method that Knochen is always preaching? Pretend you already have the information you want, then get the suspect to write it down. Klaus is doubtful about this.

Firstly, he already pretends that he knows more than he does. And as for a written confession, why would it be any better than a spoken one? He looks over at "Max," who droops in his chair, his breathing ragged, and decides a bit of consolation is in order.

He pushes the buzzer on his desk to summon Thedy, who enters, hips rolling, her face as made-up as a *putain's*. But she doesn't argue when Klaus asks her to fetch a little wine and a sandwich for the prisoner while he steps out for a quick lunch.

The food, which arrives within minutes of Barbie's departure, is brought in on a small tray lined with a napkin. And then, after that, "Max" is left alone. It's the first time in how many days? He can't even remember. He gazes longingly at the pork sandwich, but he knows he'd never be able to manage it—not with his cracked and broken teeth. But he picks up the glass of wine—it's a hearty merlot—and takes a sip. He shouldn't . . . a bribe of course . . . but he is so thirsty. He swallows the rest and feels a little stronger.

(15) Suicide attempt

To tell the story of "Max's" scar, we have to go back to June 18, 1940, just one day after General Pétain ordered the French army to stand down. Other *préfets* had left their posts long before, packing themselves and their families up and fleeing southward. But "Max" had remained in Chartres, believing it was his duty, not knowing that he was courting arrest.

It's simple, his captors had said when they came to get him that night: *Just sign this "protocol."* But "Max" refused because signing would have meant condemning Senegalese soldiers to death—soldiers who'd stood their ground outside the city, who'd continued to fight even after the rest of the French army pulled out. But the Germans, who'd been enraged by their obstinacy, claimed they were nothing more than war criminals who'd gone on a rampage, raping and murdering any civilians who got in their way.

When "Max" protested, they beat him, then shut him up in a cellar full of grisly remains. After a feeble attempt to escape, they even shot him. Finally, left alone in a makeshift cell in the early hours of the morning, he considered his options. It was a debate he recalled in his journal, published long after the war under the title of *Premier Combat:*

> *Whatever happens, I cannot sign.*
> *Anything rather than that, even death. . . .*
> *I know that the only human being to whom I still owe*
> *anything, my mother who gave me life, will forgive me*
> *when she knows that I acted so that French soldiers*
> *would not be treated as criminals and so that she would*
> *not have to be ashamed of her son.*

The floor of his cell happened to be littered with glass from a broken window, so it was easy. All he had to do was pick up one of the shards, slice open his throat and let the blackness envelop him.

His captors found him in time, though, and he was saved. For a while, he even stayed on in his official capacity, assisting the Germans in their administration of the city, but inside he was seething, merely biding his time until he could get to de Gaulle in London.

(16) Second attempt?

When Barbie returns from lunch, his eyes are immediately drawn to the empty wine glass. "Well, that's better," he says, looking significantly at "Max."

An electric hum has settled into "Max's" bones, pinpricks of light swim in front of his eye, but he can still sense that Barbie is keyed up . . . He's frustrated, worried, no longer so sure of himself . . . Hardly a cold-blooded interrogator . . . just an unbalanced sadist, ready to lash out at anything. The least little thing and he'd come apart . . . It wouldn't take much . . .

Marshaling what little is left of his strength, "Max" looks directly at Barbie and addresses him for the first time: "I am Max," he says through swollen lips, "but my real name is Jean Moulin." Then, exhausted, he adds: "I will say no more."

Klaus is astonished. The man has spoken. De Gaulle's personal representative. The golden goose. And he, Klaus, has accomplished it. Quickly, he follows up with his questions:

Who are your military chiefs? What is the *Armée secrète* planning? When is the invasion?

But Moulin won't answer. Klaus doesn't think he's even listening. It's insufferable, this idiotic, pointless resistance of his —as if he were the one in charge, as if he made the rules—and suddenly, before he can even tell himself to reach for a black-jack, he's hitting Moulin with it— on the head, the neck, the shoulders—until, finally, the man slides to the floor. Klaus stands over him, breathing hard, the blackjack dangling impotently from one hand. Well, it's his fault, he had a choice, thinks Klaus, giving him a kick in the ribs.

Moulin groans, but it takes another kick to bring him around. Klaus watches as he uncurls himself slowly, then gestures weakly. At first, Klaus doesn't understand—it could mean anything—but then it comes to him: he's miming the act of writing. Yes! thinks Klaus, this is what Knochen was talking about.

He helps Moulin onto the chair and returns to his desk for a pencil and piece of paper. At the top of the sheet, in the distinctive Gothic script that the Jesuits taught him, he writes "Jean Moulins." But when Klaus hands the sheet to him, he shakes his head, takes the pencil and laboriously crosses out the "s." Klaus, who is watching closely, nods: *Moulin,* yes, he's got it.

He claps Moulin on the shoulder then in a gesture that is almost paternal.

"An organizational chart," he suggests, not wanting to press too hard. "That's enough for right now."

And then he leaves the room, giving the prisoner five minutes to himself.

When he returns, Moulin is ready for him. He holds out his sheet of paper and Klaus snatches it up, eager to see what the Resistance *chef* has revealed, what secrets he's—but then he sees what's on the paper and a bolt of black fury goes through him. There is no chart. There are no names. He glances at Moulin, incredulous, then turns back to the paper.

The drawing is crude and smudged in places with blood, but there is no question who it's meant to be. The pointed chin, the protruding ears, the hair combed into a quiff: that is his face, but everything's distorted, worthless, inane, ridiculous—an unhappy accident of nature. He looks at Moulin again and lets the rage that's inside him erupt and spill over onto the man in front of him as he batters the bastard into submission, using his fists, a cosh, a length of wood—whatever.

(17) Cyanide

Lucie Aubrac is given an aspirin container full of cyanide crystals by a science professor at the university. He warns her: "Be careful—with that amount you could kill all of Lyon."

But Lucie (as she explains in her book, written when she was an old, old lady) doesn't want to kill all of Lyon. She's after just one man—René Hardy, the Judas who betrayed her husband, Raymond, and all of the others rounded up at Caluire, including of course Jean Moulin. She's heard from Raymond so she knows he is still alive, but no one has heard anything about Moulin.

Some members of Lucie's movement aren't as convinced as she is about the case against Hardy. They remind her that he's a hero of the Resistance, a saboteur who's destroyed more than 100 trains. But why then, she asks, did he come to the meeting in Caluire when he wasn't even invited? And how did he manage to escape so easily? And then, when he was finally apprehended and turned over to Barbie, why was he sent to a German military hospital where he's been all this time? (Such lavish care for a broken arm!)

There's no way of getting inside that hospital—security is too tight—but Lucie is resourceful. She mixes a bit of the cyanide with some jam from her kitchen and funnels it into a little glass jar—a single serving, not enough to share. Then she packs it up with other foodstuffs and sends it off to Hardy, a thoughtful gift from one resister to another.

After that, she goes to the morgue three or four times a week for several weeks, hoping to find Hardy's body, but she never does. It's proof, she thinks, of his guilt. He must have sensed that this unsolicited food package was dangerous, a means of retaliation. She only hopes that he didn't pass it on to some unsuspecting person.

(18) Gestapo headquarters

The plane trees of Paris are a bright golden color when Laure Moulin travels there in October of 1943, seeking clarification from the Gestapo. It is an arduous undertaking for a provincial schoolteacher like herself, who, at age fifty, has never married and lives with her mother.

Nonetheless, it's essential. There is no other way to get the answers she's seeking.

Only a few days earlier, an *envoyé* of the Gestapo had appeared at their door announcing the death of her brother, Jean. Until that moment (even though there had been no letter, no visit from a courier— nothing), Laure and her mother had still hoped. They knew Jean had been arrested, but it was under an assumed name, so who was to say that Jacques Martel wasn't alive in some corner of France or Germany? But with official notification that he was dead—a heart attack, they said, suffered while being transported to Germany—Laure feels as if something solid has come loose inside her. She can no longer go about her everyday life—teaching English, caring for *maman*, just getting up in the morning—without knowing how and when her brother died.

But it isn't easy to find these things out. She applies first at

11, rue des Saussaies; then at 84, avenue Foch; then finally at 86, avenue Foch (a complete tour of all the Gestapo sites) before encountering someone helpful, in this case one of the so-called *souris grises* whose uniforms are so dowdy. The girl, whose freckled face is scrubbed clean, listens closely, then rushes off promising to find the officer who handled the case.

The young man she returns with is ridiculously tall—a bona fide Aryan with his blond hair and blue eyes—but he, too, listens politely as she retells her story. His name, as she will learn later, is Heinrich Meiners.

"I have the *dossier* in my office, but I can tell you nothing," he says as they stand together in the corridor.

"But I've come all this way," she says. "Can't you tell me anything?" Then, seeing him hesitate, she asks: "Was he at Fresnes?"

Meiners seems taken aback by this question. "No, of course not," he says as if knowing the horrible reputation of that prison. "When your brother was transferred from Lyon to Paris, he went to a *villa privée*. He was given *traitement d'honneur*."

Laure nods. She is doubtful about this, but at least it's something to tell *maman*.

"Can you tell me where he's buried?" she asks.

"But he wasn't buried," says Meiners. "He was cremated."

Laure feels the breath go out of her. This is something she hadn't expected. She had thought there would be a body, a burial place, a gravestone.

"Later, when it is authorized," he adds, "we will bring you the ashes."

Laure looks up at the young man in front of her as her eyes cloud with tears. She is almost certain this will never happen.

For a moment Meiners is silent. Down the hall a telephone is ringing. Clerks push past them carrying stacks of files. But he must see her distress because he says, "As a *homme privé*, I understand your *douleur*, but I am a German officer and my duty comes first."

Laure fumbles in her purse for a handkerchief and wipes her eyes with it. All she wants now is to get away from this place, to board the train and be at home with *maman*. But as she turns to go, Meiners touches her on the elbow. "Your brother believed he was doing his duty," he says, in a less official, almost personal tone of voice, "but you have to understand that he was working against us."

Yes, thinks Laure. That is the way it always goes: nations quarrel and then young men die. But she will not let her brother die. He may not have a gravestone, but she will take it upon herself to tell his story, his complete story. She'll talk with his colleagues, his friends, the people who loved him, his rivals even—with everyone in fact—so that whatever he did in secret can be acknowledged by history.

The biography Laure subsequently wrote about her brother doesn't answer all our questions—who betrayed him, for instance, or how and where he died, or why he wasn't kept alive as a hostage at least—but her painstaking research, undertaken while memories were still fresh, is one of our most trustworthy sources. Jean Moulin, whose best-kept secret was always himself, may be unknowable, but his sister's account brings us closer to him than anyone else ever has.

(19) Souvenirs

Years later in La Paz, where the South American sun is always too bright, Regina Altmann mostly keeps to herself, hiding behind the pulled shades and closed drapes that keep her from looking out. She tries not to dwell on the past and on how much better things were then, but there are times when she gives in and goes through her box of souvenirs: the certificate she'd received in cookery and home economics while still a teenager, the letters Klaus sent her when he was stationed in France (not so many of those), photos of their daughter that were taken when the two of them were living in Trier with his mother.

These are "happy" keepsakes, but sometimes, such as when she's cleaning her husband's office, she'll run across something else—a threatening letter that Klaus has received or a newspaper clipping about that man Hardy who'd been acquitted twice but is still being hounded by the press. She can't understand why Klaus keeps things like that, but she leaves them alone because he'd be angry if she didn't. But when she finds the drawing that someone did of him—a caricature really—she doesn't hesitate to throw it away. He asks her about it later (hasn't she seen it? Didn't she know that he wanted to keep it?), but it was too frightful to look at, much less keep. Even now she shudders to think about the monstrous head with its shovel-like chin and ears like a gorilla's.

And besides, there was blood on it. She didn't want to have something like that on her hands.

THE MAN WHO WORE VIOLETS

COCHABAMBA, BOLIVIA - MID-1970S

She had seen him on other mornings at the Café Restaurant Continental: an older man, European, always neatly dressed, with thin white hair and an air of displacement, as if he had suddenly looked around and found himself in a place he didn't recognize.

Regine could relate. More often than not, she suffered from the same disorientation (those Bolivian palm trees, the pink-and-white stuccoing—so wrong, so immoderate); yet it wasn't the man's malaise that attracted her attention, it was the knot of miniature violets that he wore in the buttonhole of his lapel. Regine had never seen him without his badge of violets, and she felt—*knew*—that they must stand for something. Something so important and so intensely private, there was no guessing at their meaning.

Sitting across from Regine reading the newspaper was her husband, Klaus. He had offered her a section of the paper, but she was too nervous these days to read much of anything. It was simpler just to sit and watch people and wonder what their lives were like. Take Luis, the young man who almost always waited on them. Since the last time they'd seen him, he'd gotten his hair cut and was working on a mustache. Even with nothing else to go on, she felt certain their young man was in love.

Regine took a sip of the Café's strong, muddy coffee (she'd never get used to it, this horrible coffee) and watched as the man with the violets—she decided to call him *Herr Veilchen* (Mr. Violet)—stood and welcomed another man to his table. The newcomer was a little stooped but quite distinguished-looking—a doctor, she guessed, based on the little black bag he carried. Klaus, who sat with his back to the pair, couldn't see them, but Regine had an unobstructed view. She turned her attention to the two men, listening discreetly as they inquired after the health of the other, what the children and grandchildren were doing, how business was going and so on. What nice old gentlemen, she thought, guessing that their wives must be nice as well. She was picturing the nice wives in their kitchens or gardens, when she noticed Herr Veilchen glancing darkly at Klaus. Why? she wondered. Klaus knew a lot of people, both in and out of government, so perhaps they'd had dealings of some sort. But if that was the case, something must have gone badly awry.

She glanced at her husband eating his *saltenas* and quietly reading the paper. How ordinary he seemed: a semi-retired man in his sixties who dabbled in business and doted on his grandchildren. Yet there was so much grayness to him: whole swaths of his life were shadowy, others completely blank. Even the nature of his business dealings was murky. All she knew was that things sometimes went wrong. The currency swaps, for instance, those were sometimes problematic, though she wouldn't know about them until they'd been accosted in the street, or even at the Club. It made her nervous, all this uncertainty, the feeling that grievances were ripening all around them, ready to fall on their heads at any moment.

* * *

The man wearing the violets was actually Gustavo Stier, and he had been in Bolivia for nearly forty years. In the part of himself (his brain? his soul?) where identity was imprinted, he still considered himself Austrian, even though it had been a long time since anyone else had. Not since 1938, in fact, the year of the *Anschluss*. That was when Hitler, without firing a shot, had swallowed up Austria, while managing, at the same time, to recast Gustavo as a Jew—albeit a Jew who went to Mass every Sunday.

But he was not the only one who had undergone a change. It was all of his neighbors, too, good solid Austrians who had come pouring into the Heldenplatz, thrusting their arms out stiffly and shouting *Heil Hitler, Heil Hitler, Heil Hitler* until Gustavo felt as if he were sinking beneath the weight of their words. But it was the *Hausfrauen* who were the worst, yelping and keening and flapping their bouquets like madwomen as soon as they caught sight of their messiah in his big open touring car. Some even tried to climb inside, as if wanting to rub their flesh up against the Führer's.

Gustavo had been sickened by the spectacle, but it had opened his eyes, making him realize that, yes, he had to get out, it was now or never. The United States hadn't wanted him, or at least not for eight more years, but Bolivia had offered him refuge. He was grateful to his adopted country, of course, but more than a little distressed by the fascist scum that started to arrive after the war. He had not foreseen that. Later, someone explained to him that Bolivia was the end of the Rat Line—in other words, the new home of the *Kameraden*.

And there, sitting just one table away, enjoying his morning pastries, was one of the rats now, a man who called himself Altmann, but whose real name was Barbie—Klaus Barbie, the Butcher of Lyon.

When he'd first seen him at the Café, Gustavo had assumed that he was a German businessman, but then an ugly rumor had caught up with him and he'd started to do his own research. The man was no Eichmann, that much was clear, but Gustavo didn't care; he was still one of the faithful lackeys who'd kept the Third Reich humming. In France, Barbie had bludgeoned to death Jean Moulin, who was de Gaulle's personal representative; then, in Bolivia, he'd teamed up with the CIA to take out Che Gueverra.

Gustavo turned to his friend and nodded in Barbie's direction. "Do you know that man? The one with the bald head?"

But Frederico, instead of answering, only looked around quickly, his glance falling on a bulky young man who sat at a nearby table watching the door. Then, leaning forward, he whispered, "Careful, he can hear us."

Gustavo stared at his old friend in disbelief. They should keep quiet because of a bodyguard? What was wrong with Frederico anyway? Hadn't he been pushed out of Austria just as Gustavo had? Hadn't his family (except for one sister) also gone up in smoke?

"Don't tell me you're afraid of this assassin?" he said, raising his voice and gesturing toward the man who called himself Altmann.

* * *

Assassin? The word hit Regine like a fist in the stomach. Was he referring to Klaus? If so, it was a ludicrous claim, a complete distortion. Her husband had never had much to do with Jews.

He had been tasked with disabling the Resistance—an altogether different thing.

Across from Regine, Klaus lowered his paper. "What's wrong?" he asked, looking at her closely. "Is it your stomach again?"

Regine didn't bother answering. Her attention was fixed on Herr Veilchen. He was such a small man, quite insignificant really, but she knew he was dangerous. She felt it in her poor ulcerated gut.

"C'mon, Gin, what is it?" said Klaus, taking her hand and squeezing it.

Regine dragged her eyes back to his. "It's those men," she whispered. "The ones at that table over there."

Klaus glanced around in a cursory way. "Which men? What table?"

Regine knew he was humoring her. He had told her often enough that she worried too much, that if she didn't stop seeing Mossad agents on every corner, she'd work herself into such a state that she wouldn't be able to leave the house. And perhaps he was right, perhaps she did worry too much, but how could she help it when Nazi-hunters like that Klarsfeld woman were nosing around, throwing themselves at the newspapers and stirring things up?

"So tell me," said Klaus, "what are these men doing? Looking perhaps? Or pointing?"

"Looking," said Regine shortly, irritated by the jocular tone of his voice. Klaus couldn't see Herr Veilchen's face, but she could, and it was chilling, almost as if he'd like to see Klaus dead. And perhaps that was what he wanted. She wondered if he could be armed, and her stomach contracted at the thought of a gun. No, she told herself sternly, stop thinking like this. You'll go crazy if you don't.

To steady herself, she took a few deep breaths and wiped

her mind clean of everything but the ceiling fan slowly churning above her. Then, little by little, she let her eyes move around the restaurant, which was really very nice, almost like something you'd find in Europe. It was partly the waiters in their long aprons, partly the customers themselves, business people mostly, all of them nicely dressed. Take the woman coming in just now: she was older, probably about the same age as Regine, but much more chic, wearing high heels and a double strand of pearls.

Idly, Regine wondered what would happen if she did her hair up in a French twist and draped herself in pearls. Would she be as elegant? But then she looked down at her floral print dress (so dowdy) and relinquished the thought: no, there was no chance of that; she was a *Frauchen*, as God had intended.

Just then, Luis appeared to refill their coffee cups, and she took the opportunity to compliment him on his mustache. It reminded her of Klaus-Jörge, who had always wanted a big Latin mustache but had never quite managed it. What a good son he had been, an even-tempered and sunny child if ever there'd been one, a mama's boy who, even after he was married, still came running whenever she called. When he was killed in that unfortunate accident, she'd wanted to die herself.

Regine's attention drifted back to the neighboring table, where the elegant lady with the pearls was now sitting with Herr Veilchen. Regine could tell that she was the wife of the doctor: it was obvious from the way they were sitting, side by side, very much a unit, almost as if they were facing off against Herr Veilchen. And, indeed, that seemed to be the case since Frau Doktor was addressing him quietly but with great urgency. He listened, grudgingly it seemed, but then, all at once, interrupted vehemently. Regine tried to follow, but her Spanish was weak and Herr Veilchen spoke so quickly that the words ran together. But whatever he was saying, it was clearly disturbing to the doctor, who put his hand on Herr Veilchen's arm, either to placate him or hold him back physically.

Then, all at once, Frau Doktor's voice cut through sharply in German: "Why do you persist in seeing Nazis everywhere you go?" she asked. "It is destroying your sanity."

Herr Veilchen received her message in what seemed like stunned silence, sitting there and blinking his eyes as if she'd scratched him with a poisonous dart. But then, abruptly, he leaped from his chair and, raising his arm shoulder-high, pointed directly at Klaus.

"This man was head of the Gestapo in Lyon," he shouted, looking around the restaurant as if he were a judge rendering his verdict. "*Le boucher de Lyon*, that's what they called him."

The restaurant went silent. No conversation. No clatter of dishes. No scraping of chairs. Regine looked at Klaus in alarm. She knew what he was like when someone insulted him: he simply couldn't take it. Where the rage came from, she didn't know, but there seemed to be something inside him, a sensor so extraordinarily delicate that the least bit of jostling was enough to trigger an explosion.

She watched nervously as he folded his newspaper and laid it beside his plate with apparent regret. But Regine knew her husband. This reluctance of his was not really reluctance, but part of his strategy, a way of prolonging the suspense, of confusing his opponent.

Slowly Klaus rose to face his accuser. "Don't you know enough not to point your finger at people?" he said, his voice deathly quiet.

Gustavo looked into Barbie's darkly flushed face. "But that is how one points at a *Bluthund* like you," he answered, buoyed by the wave of adrenaline that surged through him. But then, feeling something vise-like on the elbow, he looked down to see the bodyguard's hand clamping him tightly. Before he could shake it away, though, or even try to, Barbie had waved the man off.

So, Gustavo reflected, this would be between the two of them, the persecutor and the persecuted. Thirty years ago in the Third Reich, a Jew would not have had a chance against a Nazi. But they were in the New World now and there was no longer a Nazi state or a Hitler, or even a uniform with runes on the collar, to lend Barbie power; whereas Gustavo had all the members of his extinguished family behind him. Formerly, their presence had been like a dark mist weighing him down, but now they were like a stiff wind blowing at his back, urging him forward.

Barbie stepped closer, so close that Gustavo felt the man's breath on his skin, but he didn't flinch.

"I could slap you!" the old Nazi said, still in that hoarse, almost theatrical whisper.

Gustavo almost laughed. A slap? That was the best The Butcher could do? Had he forgotten his repertoire: yanking out fingernails, attaching electrodes, half-drowning his victims in the *baignoire*? Gustavo pushed his face into Barbie's and dug deep into the pit of his hatred. *"Sie geben keine Nackenschüsse mehr?"* Aren't you shooting people in the back of the neck anymore?

After that, things happened so quickly that Gustavo barely registered them: the bodyguard shoving him into a chair so roughly that it tipped over; Frau Doktor screaming; and Barbie, somewhere on the fringes, stalking away with his wife. Within moments, a pair of waiters had Gustavo back in his chair, and Frederico was beside him, feeling him all over, asking if he was all right. Gustavo nodded yes. Of course, he was all right. Everything was all right. All these years he'd been wearing his violets, but what good had it done? It had been his way of remembering those who were gone (his parents, the violin-playing sister, his two older brothers, all the rest of them), but how could anyone have known that?

Today, though, was different. Today he'd stepped out of the shadows and delivered his testimony. Barbie might be only one man, not much more than a cipher really, but Gustavo Stier had dared to look him in the eye and call him what he was: a criminal.

Glancing around the restaurant, he was pleased to see that none of the other patrons had moved. Instead, they sat there quiet, watchful, a look of shock on their faces. He nodded gravely to the table on his right where several students sat, then to his left where a group of businessmen were installed, acknowledging the service they had rendered as witnesses. Then, by craning his neck at a difficult angle, he managed a glimpse of the Barbies, husband and wife, as they hurried past the restaurant's plate glass window on their way down the street. It wasn't much—just the top of his bald head, a scrap of her floral print dress—but it was enough to ascertain their defeat.

* * *

Outside on the sidewalk, Regina threw a backward glance at the café. Everything she'd loved about the Continental—the morning bustle, the juicy *saltenas*, Luis with his fledgling mustache—was lost to her now, a simple fact that left her woozy and unsteady. She wanted to protest—*Klaus, how can you let someone treat you like that?*—but she could tell by the way he was tugging on her arm, practically dragging her along, that there was no point in pleading.

Having fled Germany in 1950, they'd resigned themselves to Bolivia—they'd make the best of it, no matter how bad it was —but what difference had it made? The war had still found them, thanks to a ridiculous little man wearing violets (Jewish of course, she saw that now), and here they were, forced to give way again. She saw what was happening, how their world was contracting—today the Continental, tomorrow perhaps the German Club—and it was awful, almost unbearable, a kind of *Lebensraum* in reverse.

BULLYBOYS

LYON, FRANCE - 1985

One of the biggest challenges of my life, both professionally and personally, came totally out of the blue. Although I was a practicing psychiatrist at the time, I wasn't a forensic psychiatrist, nor was I the kind of person who sought out difficult cases. But I was on staff at a teaching hospital and generally well thought of by my colleagues, the result, probably, of staying in the background. Things are different now of course, but thirty-five years ago female psychiatrists were rare, at least in France, so I had to be careful around the men. Still, there were times when gender was an advantage. Or so Professor Glasser claimed when he called me into the office one sunny day in September and asked if I'd be willing to evaluate a high-profile defendant.

"It's a big case," he said, pausing provocatively for just a moment before revealing that the defendant was none other than Klaus Barbie, the so-called Butcher of Lyon who'd just been extradited from South America. "It would be a feather in your cap," he added, gesturing emphatically with his ever-present cigar, "a chance to get inside the mind of a Nazi war criminal."

I glanced at the ash accumulating on the cigar's tip, afraid it would drop onto the carpet at any moment. "But why not Dr Weber? Isn't he the one who usually—"

"Listen," said Professor Glasser, cutting in abruptly. "Weber's already been there. Gorin and Vedrinne, too. Three men, all of them top of their field, and what do they come back with? *He's intelligent. Sociable even. But peculiarly unemotional.*" Professor Glasser shook his large head in disgust. "Peculiarly unemotional," he repeated. "Imagine that: Klaus Barbie is peculiarly unemotional." Then, finally tapping the ash from his cigar into an ashtray, he added: "No, it must be you. A woman. You'll do better, I know."

For a moment, I sat there paralyzed. "But, really I don't think I'm the right—"

"Of course you are. Blonder would have been better, but you'll see. He'll try to impress you, start boasting about his exploits even before you open your mouth."

Grimly, I stared at my hands which were tightly folded in my lap. This was the last thing I needed—some grandiose *voyou* trying to impress me. Hadn't I had enough of that with R: always so full of praise for himself, always expecting me to fall at his feet.

"But don't you need someone who speaks German?"

"No, not at all. He's ridiculously proud of his French."

"But someone like him? Would I be tough enough?"

Professor Glasser looked at me from under his bushy brows. "Oh come now, Solange," he said, breaking away from protocol to call me by my first name. "I've observed you with patients. You're the iron fist inside the velvet glove."

I smiled at this unexpected cliché. I'd never told Professor Glasser anything about my history, but I walked around thinking he must have intuited it. He was a very astute practitioner, someone who had actually studied under Karl Jung. And yet he thought of me as an iron fist!

"So you'll do it," said Professor Glasser, leaning forward in his chair and beaming at me. "I'm sure Judge Riss will be delighted to hear this."

I couldn't help thinking, just from the way he said this, that the judge had probably been given my name already.

* * *

Within days, a crate of Xeroxed documents arrived at my office from Judge Riss. Included with them was a list of the charges against Barbie:

- The roundup of 86 Jews from the UGIF office on February 9, 1943.
- The arrest and torture of 19 people, and the massacre of 22 others, at Gestapo headquarters during the summer of 1943.
- The shooting of 42 people as reprisal killings during the years 1943 and 1944.
- The arrest of 52 Jewish children from a home in Izieu on April 6, 1944.
- The shooting of 70 prisoners at Bron in August of 1944.
- The roundup of SNCF railway workers on August 9, 1944.
- The deportation to Auschwitz of 650 people (50 percent Jewish, 50 percent *résistants*) on the last train to leave Lyon before the Libération.

For the next two weeks, I pored over the depositions the

judge had sent, absorbing them one by one, becoming so involved with the women's statements in particular that I felt as if I were inhabiting them. For the time it took me to read her deposition, I was Alice Vansteenberghe being laid belly down on a drawing room table and hit with a knout by Barbie's assistants until her back was broken. Next it was Itta Halaunbrenner, the mother who had tearfully handed her two little daughters over to the staff at Izieu because she thought they'd be safe there—except that they weren't because Barbie couldn't leave even small children alone. Then finally Simone Kaddouche, the thirteen-year-old girl who was beaten in front of her mother because neither knew the whereabouts of Simone's brothers. "Look at your daughter," Barbie had told the mother. "You're the one who's responsible."

* * *

For my first visit to St. Joseph's prison, I dressed carefully: a dark A-line skirt that covered my knees and a crisp white blouse with only the top button unbuttoned. My single concession to fashion was a pair of high-heeled boots, though even there, I'd chosen them not so much for their style but because I wanted to cover myself completely—and also because I knew Barbie was short, barely five foot six.

Sergeant Péan, a heavyset young man with a Provençal accent, met me at the front desk and hurried me through a maze of stone corridors. St. Joseph's prison had been built in the middle of the 19th century and was called, by some at least, *la marmite du diable*—the devil's cooking pot. It wasn't pleasant —the scent of ammonia, the clanging of iron doors as we passed from one section to another, the glare of the neon tubes overhead—but I had expected worse.

For his own protection, they'd put Barbie in an empty wing

of the prison that was completely devoid of anything human: no photos taped to the walls, no scraps of conversation, not even the sound of snoring or coughing. It made me feel as if I'd stepped onto a quarantine ward, which, in a way, I had.

By the time Péan finally stopped, we'd made so many turns that I was completely disoriented. Standing there, panting a little after my sprint, I tried not to gawk at the prisoner who was sitting on the edge of his cot, hands folded in his lap. I had studied his photos in the newspaper so I recognized him—he was old and bald and had a bit of a potbelly—but I was still surprised. I don't know what I'd expected, a monster perhaps, but he wasn't much different from any other seventy-three-year-old man you'd see strolling the streets or whiling away his time playing *pétanque* with his pals.

Péan threw open the gate to the cell. "You can step in now, Dr Louvier," he said, but I hesitated, transfixed by the stone threshold before me. Once I crossed it, I'd be alone with *him*. Nervously, I glanced at the walls, entirely blank—a window, high up, unreachable—and the bed, disconcertingly dominant in that small space. It was only a bed, the plainest possible, but it brought to mind other beds, in other small quarters, where I'd been forced to endure whatever "games" R could devise.

Péan must have sensed my panic. "Don't worry," he said. "I'll keep an eye on you." And he pointed to a chair which stood in the corridor opposite Barbie's cell.

I nodded. To have a third-party present was a violation of the trust that existed, or ought to exist, between patient and doctor, but I couldn't bring myself to send Péan away.

The moment I entered the cell, Barbie rose from his cot, almost as if he were a host inviting me into his home. And, yes, thanks to my boots, we were even in height. Tentatively, he extended his hand, but I was so unnerved by this unexpected gesture that I couldn't help backing away. Once again, though,

Péan came to my rescue. "C'mon, Barbie," he shouted, "you know the rules. No physical contact."

Barbie gave a quick nod—whether in acquiescence to Péan or in deference to me I couldn't tell—then gestured to the only chair in the cell, a folding chair which had probably been brought in especially for my visit. He seemed to be saying, *Look how civilized I am, how refined.*

But the chair was so close to his bed (so close that our knees would have touched when we sat down) that I had no choice but to move it farther back. He watched impassively while I did this, then waited for me to sit down before sitting down himself.

I could sense then the roles we'd be playing: me, the hapless psychiatrist, and Barbie, the courtly old gentleman. R had been "courtly," too, always pulling out chairs for me and taking my arm in public, then bashing me in private. But it was all part of the same thing, an assertion—an over-assertion, actually—of masculinity, a way of saying, *Look here, little woman, I'm in charge.*

Fixing my gaze an inch or so above the bridge of Barbie's nose, I introduced myself as a clinical psychiatrist from the Université Hospital of Lyon who had been asked (I didn't want to say ordered) to meet with him a total of three times. Not for anything as formal as a psychological evaluation, just general observations regarding his mental well-being.

"I'll be taking a few notes," I added, crossing one leg over the other so I could prop my notepad on my knee. "They'll be shared with the examining magistrate of course, but no one—"

"Yes, yes," he said, waving away the remainder of my preamble. "The others, Weber and the rest of them, explained that." He was clearly disgruntled, but with an effort he recovered himself. "I must say, though, you're at least easier on the eyes."

I looked down at my notepad, noticing only then that the hem of my skirt had ridden up when I crossed my legs. Cursing myself—why hadn't I simply worn pants?—I uncrossed my legs and cleared my throat. "Well, let's begin, shall we?"

"Ask me anything," he said. "I have nothing to hide."

"All right then, let's begin at the beginning. You were born, I believe, in Bad Godesburg, near Bonn, Germany, in 1913."

"That is correct."

"And you lived, at least until you were eleven, in the nearby town of Udler."

He nodded again and I scribbled a bit of shorthand on my pad. My only goal at this point was to establish a baseline; that is, to observe his demeanor when simple questions were asked. Then later, when the questions were not so simple, I'd be able to watch for deviations from the "norm."

"Can you tell me a little about your childhood?" I asked.

He shrugged. "It was a normal childhood. My parents were school teachers. We lived over the schoolhouse."

"So your father was also your teacher?"

Almost instantly, his face tightened like a fist. "I'm flattered that you know so much about me," he said with a thin smile. "You must have done a great deal of research." I couldn't tell if he was being sarcastic or not, but in any case he was not the first patient who had tried to maneuver the conversation away from himself and onto me.

"Of course I've read your file," I told him, "but that doesn't make me an expert on your life. All I know is what happened, not how you felt about it."

"Felt about what?"

"Well, for instance, what it was like seeing so much of your father, not only at home but also at school?" According to the biographical notes Judge Riss had gathered from his investigators, Barbie's father had been a violent drunk, so quick to box the ears of his students or give them a caning that he'd been forced into retirement after only six years of teaching. And if that was his behavior in public, one could only imagine what it would have been like at home.

But Barbie wasn't ready to go into any of that.

"I was a child," he said, his face and voice flat. "What did I know?"

"I think children know a great deal, M. Barbie," I said, calling him by his name for the first time. "Generally, much more than the adults around them." I paused, then added, looking directly at him: "Everything that happens to them is happening for the first time. They have no filter, no protective coating, so to speak."

I'd said the same thing at one time or another to most of my patients—it was simple encouragement, a promise not to judge them—but if I'd offered Barbie an invitation, he was having none of it.

"My childhood is irrelevant," he said, his eyelids drooping.

"No childhood is irrel—" I began, but he interrupted me.

"What do you want me to say?" he asked sharply. "That it was a misery? That I was a bastard, never really belonging anywhere, always on the outside looking in?" He pointed to my notepad. "That's what you'd like, isn't it, something juicy for your notes. Oh, the shame of it, the degradation. How could I ever stand it?" He paused for a moment almost as if he'd run out of air, but then continued in a slightly less agitated voice. "When I was growing up, people were always telling me what a shame it was that my father had waited until I was three months old to marry my mother. Why had it taken him so long? If he'd done it just three months earlier, then I would have been legitimate." He paused again, his face pinched and tight. "But what they didn't know is that I would have been a hundred times better off—no, a thousand times better off—if that *betrunken* bum had stayed away forever."

I was surprised by the ferocity of his outburst: this was the unemotional man Professor Glasser had described? I waited, hoping he'd say something else, but when he didn't, I prompted him: "He was hard on you, wasn't he?" I asked. I wasn't excusing him. There are plenty of battered children who grow up to be well adjusted, but for some—those who are less resilient or stressed in other ways—abuse skews them for life. It lays the groundwork, so to speak.

But it was clear from the way Barbie seemed to retreat into himself, knees clenched, elbows tight to his body, that he had no intention of responding.

"Dr Louvier," he said in a biting tone, "you'll have to continue this interrogation some other time. You've gotten enough out of me for one day."

* * *

That night for the first time in a long time I dreamed about R: he'd replaced Benoît, my husband, or had somehow inhabited him, and was turning me over. I could feel his breath hot and stale on the back of my neck, and I knew what was coming. He'd threatened it often enough—*Someday, Little Miss Priss, you're going to get it in the ass, what do you think of that?*—and now here he was, bending over me making good on his promise . . .

I awoke with a start, my heart pounding, actually exploding inside my chest, but everything around me was quiet and dark. I reached for Benoît's shoulder, half-expecting R to erupt from the layers of bedding, naked and leering, his big teeth shining in the darkness. But, no, it really was Benoît: *his* flannel pajamas, *his* glasses on the bedside table.

But R was still there, I felt him, and when I looked up at the ceiling I saw him.

He had been, and probably still was, a good-looking man, tall and dark-haired with big shoulders and an angular jawline. Women were always staring at him, and he encouraged them, flirting with them even if they had a boyfriend or husband standing right there. It didn't matter to him. Compliments just fell out of his mouth one after the other: *How luscious you look* (for the girls who weren't very pretty), or *The way you think, it's just so amazing* (for the girls who weren't very smart), or *You have no idea what you're doing to me, do you?* (sort of a throw-away line when he didn't feel like trying). And the women, the girls, they lapped it up.

Me too.

Me especially.

* * *

The next day I spoke with the superintendent of the prison, a man named Didier who was well past middle age and had a stalk-thin body. "It's impossible," I told him. "I'll never get anywhere meeting Barbie in his cell. Please, find us some other room." He promised he would, but I ended up having to call Judge Riss to make it happen.

In this way, M. Didier, who had said he couldn't guarantee my safety anywhere else but on the cellblock, was forced to lend me his office. It was an ideal solution: I could interview Barbie behind closed doors, but Didier wouldn't have to worry. There was a small button hidden just under the lip of his desk, and all I had to do to summon help was press it. Sergeant Péan, who showed me the button and made me practice using it, said he'd be right outside the door, available the moment I pressed it.

The office itself was austere, with the same white-washed walls and glaring overhead lights as the rest of the prison, but it had the advantage of overlooking a small rose garden. I imagined that this was the superintendent's personal plot. At any rate, the roses were neatly mulched and staked, and there was even an inmate at work raking the gravel paths.

Before long, a strange rattling could be heard in the corridor, and then the hallway door opened to reveal Barbie, shackled hand and foot. Péan, who had him by the elbow, gave him a little push, and he started across the room, the leg irons restricting his gait to a slow shuffle.

I was astonished by the transformation in him. Only a week ago he had looked almost debonair in his black turtleneck, but now, just seven days later, he'd been reduced to a shrunken old man with stooped shoulders. It was a pathetic sight, but secretly I was gratified to see him cut down to size. Barbie had ruled his little thug-dom like a knight, and now here he was, barely able to walk across the room.

R used to stagger home after a night out with his pals, drunk, bleeding, the sleeves of his shirt half torn off. He didn't have to explain to me what had happened. I knew what he was like, how he'd pick fights over nothing just because he was angry and wanted everyone else to be angry, too. I understood all of that, at least on some level, but it was still a pleasure to see him brought down. If he could dish it out, then let him get some of his own back.

In the beginning, I was full of solicitation (*Oh, you poor darling,* and so forth), but I was ashamed of myself even then. How had I gotten into this mess? Wasn't I supposed to be an intelligent woman? Getting out from under R wasn't easy, but when I finally managed it I had only one goal: to construct an all-new life for myself. I don't think anyone believed I'd make it through med school—I was a little older than everyone else in addition to being a woman—but I was determined. I worried at first that I might not be dispassionate enough for psychiatry, but my training provided me with the framework I needed to evaluate patients.

In Barbie's case, there were obvious signs of a narcissistic personality disorder. Some might even have labeled him dissocial, but I thought that was a stretch. Barbie was a piece of work, no question about that, yet I doubted there was any real pathology. What I most wanted to know, however—and this was more for my own satisfaction than anyone else's—was whether or not he felt remorse.

I gestured toward an armchair that sat across from M. Didier's desk, then watched as Barbie struggled to maneuver his chains so that he could sit down.

"Are those really necessary?" I asked Péan, gesturing to the handcuffs and leg irons.

The sergeant, still in the doorway, shrugged his shoulders. He said the superintendent had ordered them "just to be on the safe side."

"Very well," I said and waited for Péan to slip out of the room. Now, finally, I was alone with my patient.

"I am sorry they're making you wear those," I said, referring to his chains, but if he heard me he made no response.

"Still, I guess you know all about chains, don't you?" I asked, moving directly into our session. Last time I had been too circumspect, too hesitant, but I'd learned my lesson and wasn't going to let that happen again. "As a matter of fact, I believe that *your* handcuffs were lined with spikes. The more resistant the prisoner, the tighter they were pulled."

He smiled at me weakly as if acknowledging a point in my favor. He looked unwell, I thought, with dark rings under his eyes, an unhealthy, almost gray pallor to his skin.

"And that's not all," I continued, opening the folder in front of me and pretending to consult its contents. "Witnesses say that you beat them with whips, with koshes—that you always had a blackjack in your hand."

For several moments, Barbie looked out the window, and I wondered if he was admiring the roses, but when he turned back I saw that his face had hardened into a mask. "They had no one to blame but themselves," he said. "All they had to do was tell me what they knew. Then they could have gone home. They could have saved themselves."

I looked at the podgy little man in front of me, appalled at the ease with which he was able to shift the blame onto his victims. But it had been no different with R. His excesses were always my fault: I'd left dishes in the sink, or I'd gone to the market in a see-through blouse, or I hadn't been nice enough to his friends (or in some cases too nice). Nothing was ever right. I was always in the wrong.

"So I guess it was their fault when you injected acid into their bladders, or pushed three-inch-needles into their lungs, or sicced your dog on them . . ." I paused, waiting for Barbie to respond, but his face was blank.

"And the *baignoire*," I continued, "that was your specialty, wasn't it? Pushing people's heads under the water until they were on the point of drowning, then pulling them out and giving them one more chance to talk. But if they didn't, then it was back under again."

Barbie considered me coolly. "How should suspects be questioned?" he asked. "If we'd relied on the courts it would have taken months."

"But your way . . . to dispense with all legalities? Is that right?"

"Was it legal to shoot German soldiers, to blow up one of their *bierstubes*?" he said, then paused. "Well, was it?"

I didn't know what to say to this. There was something

wrong with his argument, but I couldn't come up with a response.

"You seem quite well informed," he continued, "but did you know that *résistants* were told to keep quiet for the first twenty-four hours? That gave their networks time to limit the damage. Whenever somebody was arrested, they'd go to work right away alerting contacts, shutting down safe houses, changing the mail drops. They could do this in a day, even less. So if we wanted actionable information, that was all the time we had. Just twenty-four hours." He paused for a moment, then added: "So I ask you, what would you have done in my place?"

"It doesn't matter what I would have done," I said stiffly. "We are not here to discuss me."

"*D'accord, d'accord,*" he said lightly, backing off, even smiling a little. "But honestly, do you think the French were any better? Whatever we did to them, they turned around and did to the Algerians." He was referring to the Algerian War of Independence in the nineteen-fifties, a conflict I barely remembered. "The *baignoire* in particular, that was a favorite of theirs," he said, pausing rather theatrically before adding: "So you see, I am not a criminal. I am a soldier. A good soldier."

I made a show of glancing at my watch. The hour had not quite elapsed, but I'd had more than enough. "I'm sorry," I said, closing my notepad on which I had written nothing, "but we are out of time for today."

A smirk flickered across his lips. "Of course," he said as I pressed the button to summon Péan.

* * *

I stayed late at the office that night, rereading depositions and studying the handful of photographs Judge Riss had sent. Most were of victims, but a few were of Barbie himself.

In the first, he is pictured in uniform, looking smug, his face somewhat like a ferret's. In the second, a 1948 mugshot taken by American intelligence, he looks dodgy and down on his luck, his face stubbled and his hair mostly gone. But in the third, a photo taken just eight years before, he looks different. It's his eyes, of course, and the way they say, *Please, please, please.*

R had the same kind of eyes: always sad, always wanting more. Nothing you could give him was ever enough. It was always: *Do you love me? Are you sure? Tell me again.*

I'd go crazy trying to convince him (always saying, *Yes, yes, yes,* and trying to get him to calm down), but all he'd say back was, *Then get pregnant and prove it.* It was the only "love" he'd accept. And if I tried to change the subject or jolly him out of the idea, he'd get mad and threaten to find my birth control pills and destroy them. *You don't think I'd make a good father, is that it?* he'd bellow, sounding like a bull with a pitchfork stuck in its side. I never answered that because what could I have said?

And besides I didn't want to set him off.

* * *

When I arrived at M. Didier's office the following week, it looked almost homey. The week before, his desktop had been empty, but today it was crowded with personal items: photographs of his family, a pipe and ashtray, even a small bouquet of roses that must have come from his garden. Did he cut them himself? Well, perhaps. At any rate, they were lovely: some yellow, some pink, all of them just beginning to unfold.

I thought about clearing off the desk. I always kept my own consulting room as bare as possible just to ward off distractions. But these traces of M. Didier somehow felt like a gift, as if he'd left them behind to lend me support.

I sat down at the desk and picked up one of the photos. In

the center, M. Didier stood next to a woman—Mme Didier surely—who was white-haired and kind looking, while their grown children, together with spouses and babies, arrayed themselves on either side. And though none was particularly striking, they were so charming as a whole that I moved the picture closer just so I could see it better. Then I put the vase of roses next to it, creating what might have been a small shrine, or more to the point, a modest buffer between me and the Butcher.

Before long I heard the dungeon-like sound of chains in the corridor, and then the door opened to reveal Péan who gave me a sympathetic smile before shoving his prisoner into the room.

As I watched Barbie struggle across the floor and sit down, I thought he looked even older and sicker than before. He seemed worn out, not just tired, but exhausted, and he moved as if every joint were inflamed. It had been raining for days now, and I wondered if his cell was damp. But heating a wing of the prison for a single prisoner, especially one like him, was probably not a priority.

"*Bonjour*, M. Barbie," I said. "*Comment allez-vous?*"

"*Comme ci, comme ça,*" he said in a noncommittal tone of voice. His face, I noticed, was covered with stubble. He hadn't even bothered to shave? I was surprised.

"So, our last session," I said. "And since it is our last one, I wonder if you could help me to understand, just for my own benefit, what led you to seek out a career in the SS." I was being very direct, but our time was limited. I didn't want to waste it.

He shot me an exasperated look and I added hurriedly, "I'm just curious, that's all. Because there were other options. The Wehrmacht, for instance, or with your perfect vision the Luftwaffe." I paused, then added: "Or university. You were a Gymnasium graduate after all, you had your *Abitur*. Not only that, but you were good at languages."

He gave an ambivalent shrug of his shoulders, but I could tell that I'd touched a sore spot. "University was impossible," he said shortly, the broken blood vessels in his cheeks flaring up and turning purple. "My grandfather made sure of that."

"Your grandfather?"

"Yes, my grandfather," he exploded. "That *alter Blässhuhn* wouldn't give me a pfenning after my father died. He said I didn't deserve it, that I had no rightful place in society."

Judging by the emphasis he placed on it, I had no doubt he'd preserved the phrase verbatim. It was a cutting remark, awful really, yet another boy might have been able to slough it off. But Barbie had probably nursed it for years, his feelings of personal worthlessness expanding in tandem. No wonder the National Socialist German Workers' Party would have seemed like a refuge to him.

"That must have felt very unfair," I said. "What your grandfather did, I mean."

Barbie snorted in derision. "The old fool always acted like he had no idea who my real father was, but that was *Kuhscheisse*," he said, a muscle in his jaw jumping. "We lived in a very small town. If somebody besides Nikolaus Barbie had been my father, he would have heard about it. Everybody would have. And my mother—even though she had no idea whether the *Arschloch* would marry her or not—still named me for him. If that's not proof—"

He paused to catch his breath, then went on.

"So for three months I was Anna Hees's bastard child, but so what? Willy Brandt was born the same year I was and he was a bastard too, but nobody ever seemed to care about that. They even gave him the Nobel Peace Prize. But me, I was thrown away like some piece of trash."

A petal from one of the roses had fallen onto the desk. I picked it up and stroked it a little, feeling its soft, almost oily surface. "So if you'd been able to continue your education," I asked, "what would you have chosen?"

Barbie was quick to answer. "I wanted to study law. That was always my dream." I nodded and he went on. "Herr Horrmann said that the SS would provide legal training." His voice, even now, after fifty years, sounded pathetically eager, as if this were something that might still happen.

"Herr Horrmann?" I asked. I didn't recall his name from the files.

"He was the Nazi Group Leader in Trier where I went to school. He took me under his wing, let me do a little work for him in the office."

"What sorts of things did you do?"

"Oh, the usual. Errands mostly," he replied, his response so clipped I thought he must be glossing over something.

I waited, and finally, after shifting uncomfortably in his chair, he added, "You have to understand . . . I mean, there were elements in Trier, among the clergy especially . . ."

I had no idea what he was talking about. "So what were you exactly?"

He hesitated for a moment, then said, "A voluntary helper."

I was taken aback. I knew enough to know that "voluntary helper" was a common euphemism for *Vertrauensmann* or *V-Mann*. And Barbie, having been a student at a Jesuit Gymnasium, would have been ideally situated to collect the kind of information that Horrmann and his bullyboys wanted. It was vile and pathetic—pretending to be a good Catholic boy while informing on your teachers and classmates—but it still seemed strange that a man like Barbie, who had gone on to do so much worse, would be embarrassed by what was essentially snitching.

"Herr Horrmann, was he something like a father to you?" I asked. "A good father, I mean, the opposite of what your real father was like."

Barbie's response was immediate. "Ah yes, my 'real' father," he snarled. "Now there was a specimen for you."

"How so?"

He threw me one of his withering looks—so much a part of our parlance I hardly noticed—but then, inexplicably, something shifted and he began talking about his past, sounding like almost any other patient in therapy. "I was just six years old when my father came back from the trenches," he started, his voice so low I could barely hear it, "and I couldn't understand . . . I mean, up until then, it had been just the two of us, my mother and me—and Oma of course because during the war we lived with her."

He glanced away then, toward a corner of the room where M. Didier's beige trench coat was hanging from a hook. Recognizing this as a bid for privacy, I, too, looked away, focusing on a thin crack near the door which reminded me of the letter "Z."

"It was stupid of me," he went on, "but I guess I thought it would always be like that. Even when Mutti said the war was over and *Vater* would be coming home—you know, living with us—I still didn't think that it would be . . . like it was." He laughed a mirthless laugh. "And I tried so hard to be good. You have no idea how hard. My goal—really, it's not exaggerating— was to be the best little boy in the world . . ." His voice trailed off then and he looked back at me warily, almost as if he'd been caught doing something embarrassing, picking his nose perhaps or scratching his groin.

"But being the best little boy in the world didn't get you anywhere, did it?" I said, urging him to confront his own victimhood.

"No, Dr Louvier, it did not," he said harshly, almost as if I had pried the confession out of him under duress. And for a moment his watery blue eyes took on a malevolent gleam, becoming what some of his victims, in their depositions, had called "serpent eyes."

"You think I should be ashamed," he continued, "but I've never had any regrets. I'm proud of having commanded one of the best corps in the Third Reich." He paused briefly, then added: "And if I should be born 1,000 times, I would be 1,000 times what I have been."

I was startled by the glibness of this little speech. "Surely you don't mean that?" I said, giving him a chance to recant.

But he only said. "I had a difficult duty to do, and I did it."

Repulsed, I looked down at the photo of the Didier clan. Yes, family, I thought, it's the single most durable unit of humanity. You can shed almost any other obligation (country, church, party), but not your family. Even after everything else is gone, family remains. It is almost always inviolable.

I looked over at Barbie who was slumped in his chair with his eyes half-closed, and for the first time I wondered if he'd make it to his trial. Perhaps he would die before the first witness could even be called.

"M. Barbie," I said loudly enough to rouse him, "our time is almost up. But before we close, there's something I'd like to ask you." He looked at me suspiciously, but I went on: "You have lived an exceptional life—"

He started to protest, but I was adamant: "No, you have, and I think you owe it to history to share what you know." I paused, looking out the window at the sky which had turned a dark shade of purple. "It won't make up for the pain you've caused, but it's a service you could provide."

But he only scoffed. "People already know too much. I have nothing more to add."

"But you have a daughter, Ute. And there are three grand-children as well. They're young now, but they'll grow up, and then they'll be asking about you. They'll want to know what your story was." I paused, waiting for him to look at me before I went on. "Surely you must have something to say to them."

For several long moments, Barbie was silent, leading me to believe that he was considering what I'd just said. But instead, he was thinking of something else entirely.

"I always sleep with the light on, did you know that, Dr Louvier?" he said, his voice almost wistful. "And do you know why?"

I shook my head.

"Because I am afraid of the dark."

He chuckled dryly. "It's amusing, isn't it? I was the one who threw prisoners into the cellars at the École de Santé. It was pitch black down there and damp. They had to sit chained to the wall. Sometimes they even had to stand until I called for them." He looked up. "And now, whenever I try to sleep with the light off, that's where I am. In the cellars of the École de Santé."

With his chains rattling a little, he placed his hands on the edge of the desk and leaned forward. "You see, one becomes tough when one is young. But I don't think I could do the same today."

It was not a confession. It was nothing, I knew that, and yet . . .

Outside, there was the crack of thunder and then, a minute or two later, a sudden downpour.

"*Tenez*, it's really coming down, isn't it?" I said, nodding toward the window and watching as the rose bushes writhed in the wind.

Perhaps M. Didier had heard the weather forecast and that's why he'd decided to cut a few of his flowers and bring them inside.

I studied the bouquet in front of me, then idly pulled one of the roses out of the vase. In company with the others, it had seemed yellow, but on closer examination I saw that its petals were actually veined with maroon. How subtle nature is, I thought, never a single color but always a combination. I lifted the flower to my nose and breathed in its sweet smell. No perfume could match it, I thought, about to return it to the vase when I looked up and saw Barbie watching me.

"Can I smell it too?" he asked, his voice hardly above a whisper.

It was a modest request, the kind a child might make, but at that moment it was beyond me. Even looking at him was more than I could bear (that old pathetic face! those sad pleading eyes!) and involuntarily I turned toward the window, focusing instead on M. Didier's roses which were being battered by the storm. The moment seemed endless—just how long I couldn't tell—but then I heard Péan pushing his way through the door and I looked up.

"It's about time, Dr Louvier," he said. "You're way over the hour, or didn't you know? If you hadn't pushed the button just now, I would have come in here myself just to see what was going on."

"I pushed the button?"

"Yes, just now."

"Oh," I said, not quite believing him. Had I pressed the button without realizing it? Well, perhaps I had.

Péan hooked his hand under Barbie's armpit and yanked him to his feet, then hustled him toward the door. I should bid him farewell, I thought. This was our final visit after all, and I'd never see him again. But instead I did nothing, just sat there listening, first to the heavy door as it swung closed behind him and then to the sound of his chains being hauled over the stones in the corridor.

* * *

When the conductor asked me for my ticket on the train that night, I reached into my coat pocket and pulled out not just the ticket, but also M. Didier's rose. I must have stuffed it there on my way out of the office. It was a sad little artifact now, squashed and limp, but when I lifted it to my nose it was as fragrant as ever.

R used to bring me roses after a fight. He'd pick them up at the grocery store or buy them from some guy on the street. They never lasted, though, just bowed their sad little heads and dried up. And if they smelled at all, it was like a refrigerator case. Yet I never refused them.

Even covered in bruises, I'd take them and put them in water. I had to. He just looked so sad I couldn't help it.

The train swayed to a stop—my stop—and I gathered up my things and pushed my way into the aisle. Outside on the platform, though, I felt something sharp digging into the palm of my hand and looked down to see that I was still clutching the rose. It was nothing but a soggy remnant now, but its thorns were still sharp. While other commuters surged past me, their shoulders bumping into mine, I stood there rolling the rose's stem idly between my thumb and forefinger, only half-aware of the tears stinging my eyes.

All that training, all those years of seeing patients and writing up notes, but where had it gotten me? I was still the same soft-hearted (soft-headed!) sucker I'd always been. Anyone, no matter how malignant, could con me. And without another thought, I tossed the poor abused rose into the nearest refuse bin.

He'd wanted to smell it and I had felt bad about not letting him, but at the last moment I'd denied him. The thought of his evil old nose burrowing its way into the delicacy of those petals was simply too awful. No, the chains were right, the flower was wrong.

The rain had slackened a little now, but the wind was still fierce, rocking the traffic light which hung like a lantern over the intersection and tearing the last of the autumn leaves from their branches. Tomorrow, gardens throughout the Rhône would be in shambles, their brightly colored chrysanthemums torn to bits, the stems of their asters bent and broken in a silent submission to the winter that would soon overtake us all.

BRIEF ENCOUNTERS: A SURVEY
WITH ELEVEN RESPONDENTS

London, England - 1992

Leo Marks, *the first of my interviewees, greets me with a pot of hot tea (much appreciated on this damp November day) and an assortment of store-bought biscuits. Marks, who is seventy-two, has ruddy cheeks, a large fleshy nose, and a staticky fringe of white hair which rings his bald head.*

I ask him about his work with the SOE, the WWII intelligence service set up by Churchill, but he seems reluctant to say much of anything, even though he was head of the codes office which gave radio support to covert agents. At first, I think his reticence may have something to do with the Official Secrets Act —or even perhaps the fact that I'm French—but, no, he wants me to wait for the publication of his memoir ("Between Silk and Cyanide," he announces with an eyebrow waggle). I prepare to put up a fuss, but his mood lightens when I tell him that I'm mainly interested in Jean Moulin.

"Ah, yes, Jean Moulin," he says, his baggy face cracking into

a smile, "there was only one of him," and after that he needs no
more prompting.

Keep in mind, Mr. Pagel, that I only saw him once, and it was
from quite a distance, but all the same you couldn't mistake
him. This was at SOE headquarters on Baker Street, and he
was striding down the hall with Yeo-Thomas, or Tommy, as we
called him. The two of them looked so much alike they could
have been brothers. The same height, the same solid build.
There was just something about them, the way they radiated
confidence and determination. You couldn't help but be
impressed.

No one had heard of Yeo-Thomas then. Later, of course, he
became famous. *The White Rabbit*—perhaps you've read the
book. But Jean Moulin was already a legend at SOE, though we
knew him only by his code name "Max."

When he came over to London from France in 1941, he
interviewed with both de Gaulle and the SOE. He would have
been a boon to our organization, no question about it. But he
ended up going with de Gaulle. Understandable, of course.
Still, it was a strange pairing. Moulin was a Republican, very
left-wing and as anti-clerical as they come, while de Gaulle was
the opposite, a conservative who went to Mass every Sunday.
But obviously they hit it off. You heard a lot of tittle-tattle in
those days: how Roosevelt couldn't stand de Gaulle, how Passy
loathed d'Astier and so forth, but never a word about de Gaulle
and Moulin. They were so close they might as well have been
one person. Or that's the way it seemed.

But that might have been Moulin's downfall. De Gaulle
made him his personal representative and gave him complete
responsibility, which didn't sit well with everyone. I'm an
Englishman so maybe I'm prejudiced, but the Resistance in

France was pathetic, especially when it came to security. And totally fragmented, with one group here, another one there. No one liked or trusted each other. Yet Moulin was supposed to bring them together and make them toe the line. That was his mission.

Not that he wasn't up to the task. He was. But he paid the price, and it was a big one....

What do I mean? Well, let's just say that the moment he jumped from that plane he was doomed.

There was no helping him then.

Paris, France - 1993

André Dewawrin, better known, at least during the war, by his pseudonym, Colonel Passy, is waiting for me at Les Deux Magots. It's a lovely spring day and the terrace is crowded with tourists. But if Passy feels out of place it doesn't show. He's in his eighties now and has been retired for some time, but having been a banker for most of his civilian life, he probably feels just as comfortable in his pin-striped suit as the tourists do in their blue jeans and sandals. He is a tall man and his legs, crossed at the knee, are as thin as sticks. And though he sips his wine with leisurely contentment (he is a connoisseur, he tells me), there is still something about him—a heightened sense of awareness, a constant scanning of his surroundings—that brings to mind his role as de Gaulle's intelligence chief.

I first saw Moulin at Ringway. You know, the parachute school near Manchester. He was training with British paratroopers, and for someone his age—he was in his forties after all—it was rough. Of course, he prided himself on being *sportif*, but paratrooper training is nothing like skiing in the Alps. Take the "flying angels," for example: you had to jump from a spring-board over a wooden horse without anyone there to catch you. A few hours of that, and even men in their twenties were on the point of collapse. But Moulin hung in there.

I don't know if you know, but his father pulled strings to keep him out of the fighting in World War I. So it's my guess he was trying to prove something. If he could jump out of an airplane, it might make up for his never having charged into battle.

As I said, though, the training was arduous. One day I even saw him in a corner of the gym vomiting from fatigue. I didn't have much hope for him then. I thought he'd join de Gaulle's gaggle of acolytes and stay in London doing paperwork. He'd been a *préfet* after all, so he was more used to hosting banquets and balls than living undercover.

I was wrong about his chances, though, because Ringway ended up passing him. Just how I don't know. But in any case he ended up going to France and living the life of a spy.

Vanves, France - 1993

Francette Pejot-Jarre offers me sherry when I arrive at her apartment, which is in Vanves, the most densely populated suburb of Paris. The apartment itself is airy and bright but so aggressively modern with its open floor plan and exposed pipes that I can't help feeling a little sorry for her.

Mme Pejot-Jarre, who was known as Marianne during the war, is from Lyon and was a jeune fille de bonne famille. I don't think she or her sister, Raymonde, ever wanted for anything, not even after their parents died in 1942. They could have sold the family business then— everyone was advising it—but they were both in their twenties and had worked in the shop off and on from the time they were twelve or thirteen, so they decided to keep it and run it themselves. They even opened it up as a storage place for the Resistance. And they were just as generous with their apartment which was turned into an office.

Mme Pejot-Jarre was a beauty in her day with strikingly dark hair and eyes and a figure that even she describes as sumptuous. Time has had its way, though, and today, at age seventy-nine, she's as round as a dumpling and her hair has faded to gray. But it's clear that she likes having a "gentleman caller." Her eyes sparkle as she talks to me, and from time to time she puts a hand on my forearm or even my knee.

We both enjoy this.

Only a week after our parents died, some friends asked Raymonde and me if we'd like to join the Resistance, and of course I said yes. I didn't even think about it. Raymonde was afraid, though. She thought it was too risky. But I told her, this was our chance, maybe the only chance we'd ever have, to do something important. And, besides, we'd be working for Jean-Pierre Lévy, and he was a very impressive man—the head of a group called *Franc-Tireur.* I was thrilled to be included, and after a little, Raymonde was too.

Our shop, which was called *La Lingerie Pratique,* was famous for its laces and luxury trimmings. I think that's why Jean-Pierre asked if he could store things there, because who would ever suspect a lingerie shop of hiding contraband?

Max used to come there quite often, but we didn't know his actual name or how important he was. He was quite unassuming and always looked a little shabby. His overcoat, I remember, was almost threadbare.

And there was something the matter with his voice. He was

always hoarse and sometimes when he was talking to you he'd make this little choking sound. By now everybody knows about how he cut his own throat. That was in 1940 during the fall of France. He was still a *préfet* then and I think the Boches wanted him to sign off on the execution of some French Senegalese soldiers. But of course he wasn't going to do that and so he ended up being tortured. Raymonde says slitting his own throat the way he did was brave, but I think he was just so afraid of giving in that suicide seemed like the only option.

It must have been awful for him, though, sitting there in his makeshift cell in the *petites heures du matin* wondering what they were going to do to him next. But the window in his cell had shattered during the bombing so the floor was covered in shards of glass, something which might have struck him as providential. In any case, he didn't have to search for a weapon, it was right there at his feet.

Somehow he survived—one of the guards must have found him—but he'd cut his vocal cords and they never healed, at least not properly. Can you imagine, slicing so deep into your throat that you hit your larynx? Jean-Pierre told me that was why he always wore a scarf, to hide the scar.

Is there anything else I remember? Well, he had very arresting eyes—brown, but not a solid brown because there were all these little flecks of green and gold mixed in. Honestly, they were quite lovely. I mentioned them to Raymonde once, but she said she didn't know what I was talking about. I told her she needed to look more closely.

Lyon, France - 1993

My fifteen-year-old son, Jacques, comes with me to visit Colonel Paul Rivière. We are both unhappy about this, but there was no other choice. His mother, who normally has custody, is off somewhere finding herself, so he's my responsibility for the month of July. And I don't dare leave him at home. He'd only invite his pot-smoking friends to drop by. So here we are, the two of us, paying a visit to Colonel Rivière at his nursing home, which, to judge by its amenities, must be quite expensive.

We meet in the home's atrium which has comfortable seating and an abundance of large healthy plants, including a ficus benjamina so tall it could be considered a tree. My mother's hospice facility had plants too, but they were leggy and anemic-looking, an all-too-clear indication that she had come to the end of her short, sad life.

The eighty-one-year-old Rivière sits waiting for us in his wheelchair with a crocheted afghan over his knees. One look at him, and Jacques starts dragging his feet. But he freaks out completely when the receptionist tells us that Rivière is almost blind and so hard of hearing you have to shout in his ear if you want to communicate. At that point Jacques actually stops in his tracks and starts looking around. It's as if he's trying to figure out someplace else to be—the gift shop perhaps or even the nurse's station. But I pull him along, making sure to introduce the colonel not only as a hero of the Resistance but also as a Legion of Honor recipient. This, thank goodness, is sufficiently impressive to get Jacques to sit down and at least pretend to be listening.

I was a member of Combat when I met Jean Moulin. This was in Lyon, at the apartment of some fellow *résistants*. I even recall the address: 106 rue Pasteur. . . . It's strange, isn't it, to remember something like that? But when you're young everything is so vivid. Now I barely remember my own address . . .

But Moulin, yes: the RAF dropped him into France on

New Year's Day in 1942, but his pilot was off course so he ended up in some swamp. Worse yet, he'd lost track of Montjaret, his radio operator. Moulin had no idea what had happened to him. Had he been injured, taken prisoner, or what? *En tout cas,* it was a risky situation because sometimes— not sometimes, actually quite often—the locals, if they came across someone who was wounded or maybe just wandering around, they'd haul him off to the Vichy police.

What's that, Jacques? . . . No, please, M. Pagel. Let him ask as many questions as he likes. It's nice to run across someone his age who's interested. So many aren't. And, besides, it's a good question: Why *did* the French police cooperate with the Gestapo? Well, it's complicated, but what you have to remember is that Vichy France was in bed with the Nazis. Everyone, from General Pétain on down, was certain Germany would win the war. After Stalingrad, people started changing their minds, but in 1942 when Moulin arrived, the Resistance was just limping along. He was the man who got us back on track.

But, wait, you're writing a book, aren't you? You want something exciting, don't you?

Drama and so forth. Well, I have to say that our first meeting with Moulin was pretty dramatic. Just having him there, talking to us about de Gaulle and the Free French was exhilarating all by itself. But when he said he had 250,000 francs to give us, we were beside ourselves. I can't tell you how thrilled everybody was—everybody except Henri Frenay that is.

He was the leader of Combat, and I don't know what was eating him, but he just stood there, not saying much of anything. That's when Moulin took a matchbox out of his pocket and started pulling out tiny slips of microfilm. It was ingenious, the way they'd been cut to fit the exact contours of the box. Anyway, Moulin handed the first piece to me along with a magnifying glass. At first the words were just a blur, but then I could feel my heart start to pound as they came into focus. What it said, and I remember this exactly, was: "I hereby appoint Jean Moulin as my personal representative and as the delegate of the French National Committee to the zone of metropolitan France not under direct occupation." It went on from there, describing his mission and so forth, and then, down at the bottom, there was the General's signature: "C. de Gaulle."

I was speechless. We all were. This guy was for real and he had the backing of a general. Not even Frenay could argue with that.

Moulin wasn't with us long—only about eighteen months— but in those eighteen months everything turned around. Right off the bat, he created several new agencies, one of which was the *Service des Opérations Aériennes et Maritimes*, or SOAM. That was the group I was a part of. We handled all the landings from Britain, whether by sea or by air. That was hair-raising work as you can imagine. In our area alone, we had something like fifteen separate police forces breathing down our necks, plus of course the Abwehr and the Gestapo. Inevitably, we had some close calls, but never any catastrophes, *grace à Dieu*.

But to get back to Jean Moulin, it's hard to believe he accomplished everything he did. People like Frenay were always complaining about how dictatorial and officious he was, but I don't think anybody else could have taken our motley units and turned them into an army. Even Emmanuel d'Astier —and he was not one of Moulin's biggest fans—described him as a true *"homme d'état."* And it's true, he had skills that none of the rest of us had: diplomacy, organization—a vision for the future. He was the only one among us, except for de Gaulle of course, who had the makings of a Prime Minister.

. . .

Villevieux, France - 1993

Marie-Louise Wurtz is waiting for me in the library of her chateau when I arrive. She is 101 years old, by far the oldest person I have ever interviewed—or seen. Sitting in her wheelchair swaddled in blankets, she reminds me of an antique doll, the kind you sometimes see in resale shops with cracked bisque faces and frizzy mohair curls. But her eyes are bright and she extends a welcoming hand to me. Uncertain, I bend over and kiss it—I am in a chateau after all—and she beams at me, displaying a mouthful of jagged brown teeth. She has me sit down in a chair next to her, and within minutes an elderly woman appears bearing a pot of tea and a plate of small sandwiches.

After pouring each of us a cup of tea, she unexpectedly fills a cup for herself and sits down on the sofa, obviously planning to stay. I glance at Mme Wurtz and she introduces me to Lucie Brossier, the wife of a tenant. There's a certain caginess about Mme Brossier that reminds me of my mother, and I wonder if she thinks I'm after something—which of course I am.

But it's not what she thinks. I have no interest in Mme Wurtz's money, and I don't intend to pocket one of her little treasures on my way out. I just want to hear about Jean Moulin, who's been like a guiding star to me my whole life.

There's a fire in the fireplace, but the room is still damp and chilly. Nonetheless, I am charmed by its antiquated elegance. Everything in it is old: the dark wood paneling, the heavy brass andirons, the antique Persian rugs—not to mention the books, which are bound in leather so dry and cracked they look as if they'd crumble at the first touch.

. . .

During the war, we had a lot of visitors: *résistants* mostly, though a downed pilot would show up every now and again. It was just my two sisters and myself. I was a widow and Cécile and Marguerite had never married, so there was no man on the place. If there had been, well, who knows. Don't take this personally, but men, in my experience anyway, aren't much for the underdog. Present them with a bully and they gather round. How else do you explain that old goat Pétain, or Laval who was even worse? They were the ones who came up with the idea of a puppet government, they're the ones who dragged France through the mud.

But my sisters and I saw through the Boches right away. I know it's not polite to call them that anymore. We're supposed to be more enlightened. But Boches killed my husband and my two brothers in that first war of theirs, and that's not something you forget. My two sisters and I wore black for years, and we weren't the only—

What's that, Lucie? . . . Oh, yes, Jean Moulin, he's the one you wanted to hear about.

Well, he was definitely our most important guest, though you wouldn't have known it if you'd seen him that first night. We were asleep when he arrived with General Delestraint—he was commander-in-chief of the *Armée secrète*, you know—and both of them, well, they looked more like laborers than anything else. It was such a funny scene. I mean, there we were, with our braided hair and dressing gowns, and there was M. Moulin, dressed like a truck driver in his black beret and *canadienne* . . .

What's a *canadienne*? Well, it's one of those fur-lined jackets that are really warm. They're sometimes called parkas, I think.

Anyway, they were waiting for a plane to fly them to London, but there were problems so they ended up staying with us for something like a week. The plane was scheduled to land on a field at La Grange-de-Paille—it's quite close to us, Lucie can show you if you like—but nothing worked out. The weather was bad, or the plane sent to pick them up was shot down, or for some reason or other the landing field wasn't staffed.

Naturally time dragged for them, two important men like that, but they didn't let on. M. Moulin was *si sympathique, si charmant*, and so was the general, though he was a good deal quieter. M. Moulin even made a conquest of Bébé, our old Pyrenees sheepdog who was always so cross.

During the day the two of them were always busy, M. Moulin in particular. He wrote letters to some of his friends who were in prison, made sketches all over the chateau (he was quite a good artist) and even came in here to look for books. We'd be going to bed, and there he'd be, sitting by the fire in this very room with a volume of Montaigne's *Essais*. That book is still here by the way, over there on a shelf by the window, right next to the family history. I don't read much anymore, but I still like seeing it there. It's a reminder of the one time in my life when I actually did something brave.

It was so delightful having the two of them here. And when they left, General Delestraint made such a pretty gesture. I don't know how he did it—perhaps Cook helped him, it's the only thing I can think of—but he gave each of us sisters a little bouquet of violets. I remember thinking how kind that was of him, especially when he had so much on his mind. But then I was easily charmed.

Avignon, France - 1993

*When I contact Madeleine Samuel (Christiane during the war),
she insists on making me a home-cooked meal: oeufs mayon-
naise, blanquette de veau and crème caramel. I feel guilty
accepting so much hospitality from her, but she says I am the one
doing her a favor since she doesn't have many chances to enter-
tain anymore.*

*Mlle Samuel, who has never married, steers me away from
any conversation that's too personal. Nor is she willing to
divulge her age ("It's nobody's business but mine," she says flat-
ly). I'm quite sure she's close to eighty, but she certainly doesn't
look it with her trim figure and fashionably cut hair, which she
says she used to dye but doesn't anymore ("What's wrong with
gray? It's just another color").*

*After dinner, Mlle Samuel serves me coffee in the salon and
tells me about her family. She says that her father was Jewish,
but not her mother. This meant that she and her brother, Léon,
were "safe," since, according to Vichy, you had to have three
Jewish grandparents to be considered Jewish. Still, she and her
brother felt Jewish, and it was this feeling that led them to join
the Resistance.*

*She always managed to escape capture, but Léon was less
fortunate. Arrested by the Gestapo chief Klaus Barbie in the
summer of '43, he was tortured and deported. He made it back
after the war, but his health was so compromised that he died
within a year, of just what no one knows.*

I was recruited by Joseph Montjaret (or Hervé), who was
Jean Moulin's radio operator. At the time, I'd been doing
some work for the Franc-Tireur group, but only on a part-
time basis. I'd deliver messages or radio crystals or whatever

else had to get from one place to another. One day I even took a couple of pistols to a man called Claudius. I borrowed my cousin's baby for that and put the pistols in the bottom of the carriage. Just another mother out for a stroll with her baby.

When I became an *agent de liaison,* I had to travel between Vichy and Paris, which was very dangerous work, especially for someone as young and inexperienced as I was. But I was working for the BCRA by then and that's what they expected .
. .

No, sorry, I don't remember what those letters stood for— there were so many acronyms in those days. But the BCRA was de Gaulle's intelligence agency, and Jean Moulin, I suppose, was the head of it, at least here in France. I had no idea who he was, though, because Hervé was always the one who gave me my orders.

I did know a "Max," though, and one day I was instructed to go to Marseille to meet him. I've forgotten just what he was bringing me—money, probably—but I remember being irritated because he wasn't following protocol. I'd been instructed to sit at a café reading a particular newspaper—*Je Suis Partout,* I think—and he was supposed to be carrying a copy of *Gringoire.* But he'd either forgotten or hadn't been able to find one, which I found inexcusable.

I can't remember exactly what I said to him, but it was something along the lines of "It's all right this time, but remember, *monsieur,* the work we do is dangerous."

Honestly, I was so appalled by this lapse that I told Hervé about it the very next day. And do you know what he did—he burst out laughing. That's because "Max" turned out to be *le grand Patron!*

Moulin told Hervé the story too. It amused him, I think, that a schoolgirl like me had chewed him out. But he also took it as proof that his disguise was working. If I hadn't guessed who he was, then how likely was it that anybody else would?

But thinking about it now . . . well, I've wondered anyway, if maybe Moulin wasn't a bit too lax when it came to security. Don't get me wrong. He was a remarkable man. Very intelligent and incredibly brave. But the villa where he was arrested had only one door when there should have been two. And the meeting itself was hardly a secret. I know because there was a lot of talk afterwards about just how many people had gotten wind of it. It's turned into kind of a parlor game now, speculating about who betrayed Moulin. But maybe nobody did.

Maybe Klaus Barbie or one of his underlings simply heard about it at the *tabac*.

Borough of Hounslow in London, England - 1994

When Jacques learns that I'm going to London to interview a flight commander decorated five times for gallantry, he begs to come along. "Your mother won't like it," I tell him, and it's true. She'd view it as an extravagance, an attempt on my part to win him away from her. But in the end, Jacques talks her into it, and so, a week or so before Christmas, we travel to London.

Group Captain Hugh Verity is seventy-six, but he could easily pass for someone in his early sixties. With his slight build and delicate coloring, he also has the look of a proper English gentleman, which of course he is. Unfortunately, though, this only serves to bring out my insecurities. Just knowing that he was educated at Cheltenham and Queen's College, Oxford is bad enough. But worse yet, he claims to have forgotten what little French he learned in school, meaning that I have to resort to my barely serviceable English if we're going to communicate.

We are interviewing Verity at the home of his daughter-in-

law (I did not catch her name), who—though she smiles nicely at Jacques—seems leery of me, asking almost right away what news service I work for. When I tell her that I'm writing a book, not an article, she wants to know the name of my publisher. Verity intervenes, however, suggesting that a pot of tea would be welcome. When she has left the room, he apologizes for her behavior, adding that he knows how hard it is to get a book published. His own book We Landed by Moonlight *moldered at the bottom of a desk drawer for years before he could find a publisher. Since then, however, it's never been out of print.*

When Verity's daughter-in-law returns with tea and scones, he invites her to sit down with us at the dining room table, but she pointedly refuses and stomps back to the kitchen. Obviously, she has something against me, but there's really no need. My agenda is such a simple one that I think she'd understand if she knew.

Generally, I flew a Westland Lysander Mark IIIA (SD), which is a small single-engine plane just big enough for a pilot and two passengers, though you could squeeze in one or two others in a pinch. The Lysander is a good little plane, and I made so many trips in it that it felt almost like home. Our operations were limited, though, because we could fly only when the moon was full, or nearly full. And even then, you had to worry about ground fog, which could crop up at any time.

That's what happened to me one night early in '43. I was flying from the RAF station at Tangmere to a field near Bourges, which should have been easy because it's a fairly short flight. But by the time I was over the Loire River, or what I thought was the Loire, I was flying over a sea of solid fog.

I had just one passenger aboard that night who was riding in the rear cockpit. It was your man, Jean Moulin, though I didn't know it at the time. He wore a very ordinary suit and coat, but you could tell by his bearing that he was a man of some authority. He just carried himself like someone who was used to being in charge. It wasn't until after the war, though, that I finally worked out who he was.

At any rate, there was no way I could land, not with all that fog, so I was forced to turn back for England. But when I got to Tangmere, the fog was even worse there, about 800 feet thick. I didn't know how I'd be able to land. The tower said they were lighting Money flares for me, and I asked them to put up two searchlights, one on each end of the runway. Placing myself between the pools of light, I flew a race-track circuit above the runway, then lowered the plane to 300 feet. I could see the Money flares all right, but I wasn't properly lined up so I had to go round again. After repeating this maneuver eleven times, I was running out of fuel. Like it or not, I had to land on my twelfth approach. I knew the airfield was down there some-where, I just had to motor steadily down. But I cut the throttle too soon—we were still thirty feet off the ground— so we ended up crash-landing. There was a tremendous crack as the under-carriage beam snapped off, and then the plane pitched forward and went into a ferocious skid with the propeller blades leading ...

Yes, good question, Jacques.

By rights, the plane should have burst into flames. There had to have been at least a little petrol left in the tank. That's why I was so concerned about my passenger. He was stuck back in the tail section, which was now pointing almost straight up, and I was afraid he'd be engulfed in flames any minute. But when I got there, I saw that he'd been able to slide his roof back and up and climb out. I helped him jump down and apologized in the best French I could muster. It had been an awful flight and the ordinary person would have been as sick as a dog after what we'd gone through, but he was as charming and polite as could be. He thanked me for "a very agreeable flight." Even said that the flak we caught over the coast of France reminded him of a fireworks show.

It still amazes me. This was the great Jean Moulin and I'd almost killed him. Yet in spite of that, there he was thanking me.

Nice, France - 1994

Lily Manhès, who is somewhere in her eighties, meets me in the bar of the hôtel Excelsior. With its Belle Époque exterior and lacy wrought-iron balconies, the Excelsior is a well-known landmark in the center of town. Still, I have trouble believing that Mme Manhès actually chose it for our rendezvous, given the fact that it was once a regional headquarters for the Gestapo. Yet the Excelsior turns out to be perfect. There's a leisureliness about the place, and the bar, perhaps because it's the middle of the afternoon, is as quiet as a hospital waiting room.

The moment she sees me, Mme Manhès motions me over to the banquetted corner where she sits nibbling on cheese straws and sipping a glass of what appears to be Scotch—my mother's drink of choice (when she had a choice, that is). In her silky pink blouse and Chanel-style suit, Mme Manhès, is more youthful and animated than I expected, and when she greets me her smile is so broad that her entire face crinkles to accommodate it.

"You look nothing like your voice on the phone," she tells me, making it sound like a good thing and laughing a little as she offers me a liver-spotted hand. "Now get yourself a drink," she adds, "and we'll talk."

. . .

So you're writing a book about Jean Moulin? Ah, that's excellent. Of course, he's been written about before, but you want to write something a little different, something more intimate, is that right?

Oh, and I agree with you 100 percent. The women in a man's life are very important. Of course, I don't know who all of them were, but Henri and I were two of Jean's oldest friends, so we knew most of his friends, both men and women.

Henri is my late husband. He's been dead for a long time—almost thirty-four years now—but back in the '30s he worked with Jean at the Air Ministry. The two of them got to be good friends, so naturally we saw a lot of him. He was with Antoinette at that—

Antoinette? Really, you've never heard of Antoinette Sachs? Well, she was Jean's ... what would you call her? *"Petite amie"* isn't right because she was more than a girlfriend, but you can't say "companion" either because she was actually Paul Géraldy's mistress ...

Yes, Géraldy, the famous poet. I think he even called Antoinette his muse.

I can't say as I ever understood their relationship—hers and Jean's, I mean—but I'm quite certain he loved her. He even asked her to marry him once, but she turned him down because of Géraldy. I was astounded when he told me he'd proposed, especially since he'd had such a bad time with Marguerite ...

What, you don't know about Marguerite ethier? Well, this is a surprise. Honestly, *monsieur*, I'm beginning to think you haven't done your homework.

I'm only joking. Besides, you're right: how can you know if you don't ask? I'm just amazed that you haven't heard of Marguerite because she was Jean's first *grand amour*. He was completely devastated when she walked out of their marriage.

Yes, of course they were married. But only for a year or so.

One day she went off to her singing lesson as usual and just never returned. She was young when he married her—rich too, or would have been when she turned twenty-one—but it was a love match and not just on his side . . .

So what happened? I think it was Marguerite's mother. She poisoned things between them. She thought the only thing Jean cared about was money.

Honestly, I can't say as I've given it much thought, but you're right, he did have a knack for coming up with the rich ones. That's not to say he didn't love Marguerite because I'm quite sure he did. But Antoinette was wealthy too—as a matter of fact, she funded the Moulin museum they're going to be building in Paris—and then there was Gilberte, and she was rolling in money, thanks to an extremely generous settlement from her ex.

There was Colette, though, and she wasn't rich, or at least not as far as I know . . . But she was young. Too young, I thought. They met in 1942, just after he'd parachuted into France on his first mission, so he would have been forty-three then. And Colette was, I don't know, twenty-seven or twenty-eight. You can't say he was robbing the cradle, but it seemed a bit desperate on his part.

I really didn't like Colette much at first. Maybe it wasn't fair, but I pegged her as a *petite futée*—you know, somebody who was just a little too cute. She was in the process of getting a divorce at the time—and nothing was final, mind you—but somehow or other she'd gotten herself engaged, or at least semi-engaged. Her fiancé was over in London, though, doing something for the Free French, so she was more or less on her own when Jean met her.

Actually, I think she gave him rather a bad time—or maybe he was just too intense, I don't know—but at one point she gave him the slip, just disappeared for two or three months.

He was really upset about it, but finally he got a friend of hers to intercede on his behalf. So then he offered her a job managing his art gallery here in Nice, and that did the trick, it solidified their relationship. I really don't think she knew a thing about art, but Jean took her to Paris on buying trips so she probably learned a lot that way . . . How Jean ever found time for that art gallery, I'll never know. You would have thought his work with the Resistance would have taken up all his—

Was there ever anyone else? Well, goodness knows, there could have been. Jean was always so secretive that it's quite possible. And you can't say he wasn't *un bel homme*—from the south of France, you know, so more Latin than French, but definitely attractive. And very, very charming. I really did love him. Both Henri and I did.

Lyon, France - 1994

I meet Hélène Van Diévort (née Vernay) for lunch at the Grand Café des Négociants, one of Lyon's most famous restaurants. Established in 1864, it has long been considered the perfect place for a business lunch. But though the service is brisk, it retains a Second Empire ambience, with its mirrored walls, mahogany woodwork, burgundy-colored draperies, and muraled ceiling.

Mme Van Diévort, who is in her mid-eighties, says the restaurant was a refuge for her during the war when she worked for the BCRA as a secretary. "You could come in here," she says, "and everything was just as it was before the occupation. It gave you hope."

Mme Van Diévort orders the suprême de poulet, which is chicken stuffed with sweetbreads and foie gras, so to please her I follow suit. I also encourage her to order whatever she'd like in the way of wine.

Her pouchy blue eyes acquire a mischievous glint.

"How kind you are," she says, bending her head with its cap of white curls over the wine list. Then, after careful considera- tion, she chooses the Pinot gris calcaire Domaine Zind- Humbrecht, which she says is in honor of me. I don't know what to make of this. It's an Alsatian wine, so does that mean she thinks I am German? Surely not, but I don't inquire.

Pentecost was on June 13 in 1943—I remember because it seemed like such an unlucky number—and I was going to my parents' for the holiday weekend. When I happened to mention this to Tony de Graaff who oversaw the secretariat where I worked, he asked me if a friend of his could come along. He didn't mention the man's name, just said he was someone who needed to get out of Lyon for a couple of days because the Gestapo was looking for him, and Trévoux, where my parents lived, would be perfect because it was so quiet and out-of-the-way.

I was a little worried about what this mystery man would be like, especially since my parents were older and rather set in their ways. But he turned out to be very amiable. A little older than I expected—I remember that his hair was going gray—but quite nice-looking all the same.

We took the *train bleu* as far as Neuville-sur-Saône, then transferred to an *autobus à gazogène*. That was one of those wood-burning buses that came into use during the war. I don't suppose you've ever seen one—no, of course not, you're too young—but all that charcoal made it smell like a campfire, which was quite disagreeable. But for some reason I didn't mind it that day. It was a holiday so the bus was crowded, so crowded we had to scramble up on top if we wanted a ride. I don't know what was so funny about that, but I do remember laughing the whole way to Trévoux.

My parents put him up in a *petit pavillon* which was in the garden behind their house. It was perfect because he could easily escape from there if he had to. My parents were completely won over by him because he was so nice and kept apologizing for intruding on them. It was very relaxing for him, I think. He spent his time going for walks in the country and once he even went snail-hunting with my mother and me.

My vacation was not as restful as his, though, because I had to spend most of it shut up in the salon typing a report that had to be finished over the weekend. He teased me a little about working on a holiday, and I remember telling him, rather sharply I'll admit, that I had a demanding boss, and what's more, his handwriting was horrible.

I didn't know it then, but a week or so later when Tony dropped by the secretariat he told me that our houseguest had actually been Max, *le Grand Patron*. At first, I didn't believe it. If he'd been taller and more severe, maybe, but someone as nice and accommodating as he was? It just didn't seem possible.

By that time, though, he was in the hands of that monster Klaus Barbie. They say it was Barbie himself who beat him to death, and I wouldn't doubt it. Barbie was vicious, and he must have had some idea how important Moulin was. But Moulin had been tortured before. If he hadn't given in then, he wasn't going to give in to *le boucher de Lyon*.

But we'll never know, will we, because Barbie denied it right up to the end. But at least the old butcher died in a French jail and not at home surrounded by family . . . I mean, it's hard to imagine, but I suppose that even a man like that has family, don't you?

Paris, France - 1994

Christian Pineau, the most illustrious of my interviewees, was not only a prominent résistant but also a successful post-war politician who served as France's Minister of Foreign Affairs from 1956 to 1958. M. Pineau, in responding to my request for an interview, invited me to join him at Les Ambassadeurs, a venerable old restaurant located in the hôtel Crillon. It was very kind of him, but once I'm there I find the palatial setting rather intimidating. Then, in an attempt to cover my nervousness, I start jabbering away about Louis XVI and Marie Antoinette and how they were guillotined only a stone's throw from here in the place de la Concorde. I know I must sound ridiculous, like a schoolboy trying to impress his teacher, but M. Pineau, who is the soul of courtesy, nods just as politely as if he were hearing of this reprehensible deed for the first time. He even goes on to tell me about Edgar Degas, who was so inspired by the restaurant's stylish clientele that he returned here time and time again to sketch them.

Beneath the twenty-five-foot-high ceiling and enormous crystal chandeliers, M. Pineau, who is ninety, reminds me of a rotund Buddha. But in spite of the wattles beneath his chin and the bags under his eyes (all his features seem to be sliding downward), he projects a vitality I hadn't expected, so it takes very little encouragement to get him going.

I was arrested by Klaus Barbie on May 3, 1943 in Lyon, but I was luckier than most. It's true, I was eventually deported to Buchenwald, but I'd expected much worse. A firing squad, or at least some sort of torture. But even though he interrogated me for eleven hours, Barbie—except for one single slap—never touched me. I have no idea why not. After all, I'd founded the

Liberation Nord movement so I wasn't some mere courier. Yet that's what he took me for. I came in claiming I was Jacques Grimaux and when he dispatched me to Montluc prison I was still Jacques Grimaux. I've tried to figure it out. Was he simply stupid, or did I just seem like a "little man" to him?

At Montluc, I was something of a favored prisoner. They even let me keep my razor. Quite astonishing, but fortuitous since it allowed me to become the prison barber. It was an unofficial position of course, but the guards all knew about it.

I was still surprised, though, when one of the friendlier NCOs came to my cell one evening—it was the twenty-fourth of June, I'm almost certain—telling me to get my razor and follow him. He then led me to a bench in the north courtyard where a prisoner was lying unconscious. It was obvious that he had been tortured because he was in very bad shape.

"*Vous rasez, monsieur,*" the sergeant instructed me, but the order made no sense. Why shave a man who was barely breathing? But then he gave me a little shove, so I took a closer look. And that's when I saw it, the scar on his neck. I knew then that the man in front of me had to be Max. If it hadn't been for the scar, though . . . I mean, his face—it was horrible, so swollen and black it hardly resembled a face. And his eyes were completely sunken. All I could think was that someone had taken a mallet and pounded them into his skull. And he had this hideous wound on his left temple. I couldn't imagine what had caused it —maybe a hobnailed boot, but more likely a club of some sort, possibly even a two-by-four.

"*Allez, monsieur,*" the sergeant said, shoving me again. I didn't know how I was going to do it, though—running a blade over that face? How would I keep from gouging him?—but the sergeant was adamant, so I asked for some soap and water and he went off to get them.

There was a sentry standing nearby but he was paying no

attention, so I crouched down beside Max. His clothes were completely shredded and caked with blood. I remember taking his hand—it was as cold as ice—and squeezing it. There was no response, though.

When the sergeant returned with a tin cup of soapy water, I started. I did my best to avoid the worst of his injuries, but it wasn't easy, especially since my blade was so dull. Little by little, though, I managed to work my razor over his upper lip and across his cheeks and chin. My hand never stopped trembling.

By then the sergeant had disappeared and so I stayed. After all, this was de Gaulle's personal envoy. Someone needed to keep vigil.

Then all of a sudden Max opened his eyes and looked straight at me. I'd swear he recognized me. *"Boire,"* he murmured.

I signaled to the sentry standing nearby. *"Ein wenig Wasser,"* I said. He hesitated for a moment, but after a little he took the cup of soapy water and rinsed it out in the fountain. Then he filled it with fresh water and brought it back to me.

Max said five or six words in English then. I couldn't understand them, though, because his voice was so raspy and broken. But when I held the cup out to him, he took a few sips.

By then it was almost ten o'clock, and the sergeant, happening to pass by, seemed surprised to see me still there. He took me back to my cell, but did nothing about Max. I would guess he was left there all night.

Did I ever see Moulin again? No, I did not. And I wish I hadn't seen him then because now it's the only image I have of him.

But you think that you might be related to him in some way? Or at least that's what your mother led you to believe? . . .

Forgive me, I don't mean to pry, but do you mean . . . Oh, I see, that is what you meant.

No, please don't apologize. Of course I understand. It's quite natural. Anyone would want to know.

And if your mother was in Lyon during the war—I believe you said she was a hostess in one of the clubs—then she could have met him. It's even possible that she might have been doing a little work for him on the side. Moulin had a wide network of informants. Barmen, showgirls, even file clerks working in Barbie's office.

In any case, I wish you luck. Jean Moulin was a man who played his cards very close to the vest. I don't believe even his closest associate knew him all that well. But talk to a few more people. There must be someone out there who can tell you what you want to know.

Bron, France - 1994

I have Jacques with me again today. This time I asked him to come along. A mistake perhaps, but I want him to be there when I interview Mme Fassier. I've never told Jacques much about his grandmother, but for some reason he seems to think she was a famous nightclub singer. Just where he got that idea, I don't know—probably from one of my stepsister's kids—but I'm counting on Mme Fassier to set him straight. She worked with my mother at Le Lapin Blanc during the war, so she'll know the truth. And if my mother had any secrets, she'll know those too.

After picking Jacques up from school (he'll be missing geometry and lunch, but not much else), the two of us drive to Bron, a suburb of Lyon where Mme Fassier lives in a nursing home. It's run by the Lutherans and is as spotlessly clean as you'd expect— and just as oppressive. The paintings on the walls are the generic usuals: a sunlit scene with mountains (or a meadow or the seaside), or else a depiction of Jesus knocking at the door (or walking on water or hanging on the cross). And the floor tiles, though highly polished, are a dreary shade of gray flecked with a smattering of every color imaginable (green, blue, magenta, etc.). It's a stratagem which may hide a few crumbs but does nothing to brighten the hallways.

When we get to her room, Mme Fassier is sitting up in bed looking rather witchy with her long gray hair and cavernous cheeks. She is wearing lipstick, however, and a satiny bed jacket which looks almost new. But then I hand her the small bouquet that I've brought, and she lets out such a cackle that Jacques actually takes a step back. He recovers himself, though, and shakes hands with her nicely when I introduce them. Mme Fassier summons an aide to bring her a vase for the flowers, but once that's done, she's off and running, even without questions from me.

Oh, M. Pagel, what a darling you are to bring me flowers. You'd think I'd be loaded with them since my son is a florist, but, would you believe, he never brings me anything. I shouldn't say never, though, because he did send over that plant, the one on the windowsill. It's called a peace lily, I think, but it almost never blooms, and even when it does the flowers aren't really flowers at all, just these narrow white pods that look sort of obscene.

I must say, you look a lot like your mother, M. Pagel. Not as much as your son does, though. Just look at those lashes of his. And those lips, they're so full and sensu—

Oh, am I embarrassing you, Jacques? All right then, I won't say anymore. But take it as a compliment because your grandmother was very attractive. To look at her, you'd have thought she grew up in a chateau rather than a tenement. That's how elegant she was. Like a movie star almost.

You see, there were two kinds of girls working at Le Lapin. I was *mignonne*, sort of cuddly, you could say, and a born extrovert. There wasn't ever a man I couldn't talk up. So that was one type, and then there was Germaine's type. You know, glamorous, but remote.

After the war, people gave girls like us a very rough time. There was hardly anybody who hadn't done a little business with the Germans—merchants, restaurateurs, you name it—but we were the ones they went after. Traitors, they called us. It still rankles, but if you want to know the truth, working at Le Lapin was the best time of my life. We were young and pretty then and liked to have fun. Not only that, but we wore the loveliest things: long slinky evening gowns cut so low that almost everything showed and the most beautiful diamond jewelry you've ever seen. It was all paste, but no one, except maybe a jeweler, could have told that. Of course they didn't let us keep anything—it was all stored in the wardrobe room—but no one could say we weren't gorgeous. The officers who came in were simply bowled over. They couldn't get enough of—

Yes, officers. German officers. Le Lapin always catered to a very elite clientele. Never any of those pimply-faced *soldats* that the girls over in the *maisons* had to—

What? You thought Le Lapin was a Resistance hangout? *Oh, ca c'est trop beau!* Really, what would have possessed your mother to say that when it was just the opposite? No, it was Germans only: the Wehrmacht, the Abwehr, the Gestapo, whoever—

Yes, Jacques, the Gestapo. They had a regional office here in Lyon. It was the one headed up by Klaus Barbie. I imagine you've heard of him just because of that big trial a few years ago.

And don't get me wrong, he got what he deserved. But all the same, I have to say that he was always very polite when he came into Le Lapin. And he was nice to all the girls, even though it was clear right from the start that the only one he was interested in was your grandmother.

No, really, he was very stuck on her. I can't begin to tell you all the nice things that he gave her—satin lingerie, strings of pearls, even a blue fox stole. The rest of us were horribly jealous. We all wanted somebody who'd pamper us the way he did her. But most of the time, all we got were crumbs. Walking-around money, that sort of thing.

Of course Germaine was lovely, ravishing really. Thick blonde hair and a husky voice, sort of like—what is that actress, the one who married Humphrey Bogart? . . .

Yes, Lauren Bacall, that's right, that's who she was like. Beautiful, but aloof. It drove the men nuts, especially Klaus. Honestly, he was like a little puppy around her . . . You didn't say, M. Pagel, but is she still alive, your mother, I mean?

I'm very sorry to hear that. What kind was it? . . . Liver? Oh, that's one of the bad ones, not much they can do. . . . And you were only nineteen when she passed? Well, that is young. And of course it's hard to lose a mother, even if you do still have a father . . .

Oh, I didn't realize. But there are some stepfathers who are almost like fathers. Still, it must have been hard, I mean you must have wondered . . . Did your mother never say anything about who—

Just that he died during the war, that's all? And you weren't even born yet? Well, that's not much, I agree. But if it's any comfort you're not alone. There were plenty of babies back then who were born on the wrong side of the blanket—

Oh, no, don't tell me you have to go, not when we were

having such a nice chat. But come again, any time you like. And you too, Jacques. Then we could talk some more.

Lyon, France - 1994

Following my interview with Mme Fassier, I drive Jacques back to school. I know he has questions, but I keep my eyes fixed on the road. "See you later?" he asks as he gets out of the car, and I mutter something, just what I'm not sure.

After that, I head for l'Albion on rue Sainte-Catherine, a dank and sleazy street that matches my mood. Here, surrounded by kebab shops and furtive drug deals, I drink the afternoon away, trying without success to forget everything the old biddy said.

As evening comes on, I catch my reflection in the darkening glass. I will be fifty in another month, not that old perhaps, but the face staring back at me looks much older. It is also a little frightening because now that I've lost my hair the skull underneath is all too apparent. As always, though, I'm neatly dressed. They say that Barbie dressed very well. It was a trademark of the Gestapo: nothing but the finest custom-made suits for them. But I'm not a showy man. I buy nondescript suits—the plainer the better—because if you're interviewing somebody, and you want him to open up, then he needs to forget all about you.

Unfortunately, though, I haven't been getting many requests for interviews. There's a new crew over at Le Progrès, and they're not keen on free-lancers like me. I tell them that I can go anywhere now that I'm single again, but all I get is the odd human-interest story. A man in Saint Rémy who says his mother once posed for Van Gogh. An antiques dealer from Bezier who collects dental implements dating back to the time of Napoleon.

That's it, the best I can do. I thought my idea for a book would get me going again, but . . .

My book, what a joke. It was never more than a ruse, just a way of poking around to see what I could find out.

Of course, I always knew I was illegitimate. It was partly the way I looked (like no one else in the family) and partly the way my mother treated me. With my sisters she was fine, but with me . . . Well, I don't blame her—I suppose she did the best she could—but I wasn't wanted, that much was clear. She'd look at me and you could see it in her eyes, how much she wished I wasn't there.

Growing up, I pelted her with questions:

If Maurice was my stepfather, then who was my real father? Well, he was someone who'd died during the war.

Was he important? Yes, very important.

Was he a hero? You could say that, yes.

That was the most I could ever get out of her. But then one day when we happened to be in Marseille—I was seven or eight then—she stopped and pointed up at a street sign. "Look, that's the name of a war hero," she said, and she spelled it out for me: B-O-U-L-E-V-A-R-D J-E-A-N M-O-U-L-I-N. It was a moment of revelation, or so I believed, and I remember getting this fizzy feeling. I thought she was finally telling me what I wanted to know. On the way home, I asked her why he was considered a hero, and she said that he'd been a member of the Resistance, its leader actually, but that the Nazis had captured and killed him. When I tried to ask other, more important questions, such as where she had met him, she told me about Le Lapin Blanc. I realize now that she was only changing the subject, telling me about *her* war instead of answering my question. But I didn't realize that then. All I saw was Jean Moulin, Resistance *chef extraordinaire,* striding into my mother's nightclub and sweeping her into his arms.

I never mentioned to anyone that Jean Moulin was my father (I must have known better), but I never stopped believing it. Even years later, as a grown man, I was still so completely convinced that when the Université Jean Moulin was going up in Lyon I took a secret pride in its construction. I thought it was a monument to my father.

I'd been a lonely child, an awkward teenager, someone who could never connect very well with other people, but I still thought of myself as someone special. Silly, of course, but with a father like Jean Moulin—a man who could stand up to torture without revealing a single name—how could it be otherwise? Wherever I went I carried him with me. He was like a bright sunlit bubble lodged just beneath my breastbone that protected me from the indignities of life.

I wish now that I'd pressed my mother to say more, because maybe, in those last ghastly months, she might have been willing to tell me the truth. After all, she'd never made a secret of having been a showgirl. I think in a way she was even proud of it, though she must have been a little ashamed as well, or else why would she have referred to Le Lapin as a watering hole for the Resistance?

I suppose it's possible, in the beginning at least, that she didn't know who Klaus Barbie was. But how could she not have? He was the Gestapo. Everything bad that happened in Lyon during the war was because of him: the reprisal killings, the *rafles,* the torture sessions at the hôtel Terminus. If nothing else, she must have heard rumors, and if so, well . . . I mean, how could she have let a man like that even touch her? That's what I don't understand.

From my booth by the window, I watch as the streetlights come on, shedding a gauzy glow over the damp pavement. I know I should go home and drink there, but I can't muster the energy it would take to leave. Just to keep busy, I fish a legal pad out of my briefcase and start to write:

Only twenty-four hours ago, I was the person I'd always thought myself to be, but from here on out I'll be nothing but an imposter: a man calling himself Louis Pagel who hauls himself from one day to the next pretending he's just like everyone else— his colleagues at work, the friends that he meets for drinks, strangers even—but who is actually hiding within himself the traces of a monster so vile—

"Papa," a voice close to me says, and I look up.

"Jacques," I say, stunned by his sudden appearance. "How did you find me?"

He shrugs, then slides his skinny teen-aged ass onto the bench opposite me. For a moment or two, he sits there assessing me. Then, noticing the legal pad, he asks what I'm writing. "Nothing," I say, pulling the pad closer to myself.

"C'mon, Papa, let me see," he says, reaching for it, but I snatch it away.

"No," I tell him, but then he reaches for it again, and this time I let him have it. After all, there's not much point in trying to shield him now. He was there, he heard what the old hag had to say.

For a moment or two, Jacques looks at me skeptically, but then he turns his attention to the pad, squinting a little as he tries to make out my handwriting. The bar is more crowded now. Gusts of cold air hit us as the door opens and closes. Raucous laughter and shouted greetings ricochet off the walls.

Finally, Jacques looks up. "This is crazy," he says in a challenging tone I'm not used to hearing from him. "I mean, this Barbie guy, whoever he is—he was the worst? He was a terrible Nazi? He killed people? He tortured people?" Jacques pauses as somewhere in the background a woman shrieks hysterically.

"He was an evil man," I say, nodding.

"But you're not," says Jacques. He is a gangly sixteen, as awkward and half-finished and certain of himself as boys his age are. "And I'm not either."

But Jacques always knew who his father was. I didn't. Eventually, though, I'd found one. A ghostly father, sure, but I could tell myself that he loved me, or would have if he'd lived. I was like a religious zealot when it came to this "father": all my belief was anchored in him.

I don't know how much longer I have—twenty-five or thirty years, I suppose—but what kind of life will it be, always having to lug around a secret like this one? I look out the plate glass window streaked with rain and feel the blood in my veins congealing. How will I ever manage?

Will I even be able to get out of bed in the morning?

"*Allez*, Papa," says Jacques, breaking into my thoughts, "it's time to go home." He hesitates for a moment, then quickly adds, "I'll drive you."

I look at him askance. *He* will drive me? But then, before I can even reply, the kid has his arm around me and we're moving toward the door, then through it into the wind and the rain outside. We're hardly a match for weather like this, an unsteady drunk and a bantam-weight boy whose legs have outgrown him, but we lean into each other, struggling as best we can in what I think must be the direction of the car.

But then the sky above us breaks open and all of a sudden it's pouring, and the whole thing is so ridiculous, so crazy—like being in the middle of a waterfall—that the only thing we can do is look up at the sky and laugh—yes, laugh, as loudly and boisterously as we can—at the torrent we're trapped in together.

ACKNOWLEDGMENTS

I would like to thank, first and foremost, Mark Mayer, whose patient, four-year mentorship was crucial to the development of this book. His insights and attention to detail were simply phenomenal.

I also want to thank John Dalton for believing in me going all the way back to my very first workshop with him. It was his encouragement that kept me from giving up on this writing dream of mine.

Thanks are in order as well for the many instructors that I was privileged to work with: Carol Anshaw and Phyllis Moore at Ragdale; W. D. Wetherell and Sena Jeter Naslund at the Vermont College of Fine Arts; Margot Livesey and Erin McGraw at Sewanee; Percival Everett at the New York State Summer Writers Institute; and Garth Greenwell, Hugh Ferrer and others at the Iowa Summer Writing Festival.

I also want to thank Connie Hampton Connally for her sound advice. The same goes for my writing group buddies: Deborah Adelman, Tammie Bob, Bill DuPree, Tom Montgomery Fate, Kit Kadlec, Byron Leonard, Susan Messer, and A.D. Nauman. I learned so much from all of you!

Special thanks are also due to Denise Stehman, my French tutor, as well as to Jackie and Greg Stolze, Connie and Rory Connally, and Kathleen and Ray Kulla, whose encouragement and hospitality gave me time away from home to concentrate on my writing.

Thank you as well to my editor, Ben White, and everyone else at Running Wild Press who made this book possible. I am grateful that *Number 12 Rue Sainte-Catherine* found such a good home.

And finally, a big, big thank-you goes to my husband, Michael, who generously gave me the time and space I needed to pursue my writing, and to my sons, Dave and Tim, who have always been my cheerleaders!

Running Wild Press publishes stories that cross genres with great stories and writing. RIZE publishes great genre stories written by people of color and by authors who identify with other marginalized groups. Our team consists of:

Lisa Diane Kastner, Founder and Executive Editor
Cody Sisco, Acquisitions Editor, RIZE
Benjamin White, Acquisition Editor, Running Wild
Peter A. Wright, Acquisition Editor, Running Wild
Resa Alboher, Editor
Angela Andrews, Editor
Sandra Bush, Editor
Ashley Crantas, Editor
Rebecca Dimyan, Editor
Abigail Efird, Editor
Aimee Hardy, Editor
Henry L. Herz, Editor
Cecilia Kennedy, Editor
Barbara Lockwood, Editor
Scott Schultz, Editor

Evangeline Estropia, Product Manager
Kimberly Ligutan, Product Manager
Lara Macaione, Marketing Director
Joelle Mitchell, Licensing and Strategy Lead
Pulp Art Studios, Cover Design
Standout Books, Interior Design
Polgarus Studios, Interior Design

Learn more about us and our stories at www.runningwild-press.com.

Loved this story and want more? Follow us at www.runningwildpress.com, www.facebook.com/runningwild press, on Twitter @lisadkastner @RunWildBooks